The
Twelve Dancing
Princesses

and Other Tales
From Grimm

THE
TWELVE DANCING
PRINCESSES

and Other Tales From Grimm

Paintings by Lidia Postma

Edited by Naomi Lewis

DIAL BOOKS · New York

First published in the United States 1986 by Dial Books
A Division of E. P. Dutton
A Division of New American Library
2 Park Avenue
New York, New York 10016

Published in Great Britain 1985 by Hutchinson Children's Books Ltd.
Printed and bound in Belgium. ☒
First edition
US
10 9 8 7 6 5 4 3 2 1

Library of Congress Cataloging in Publication Data

Grimm, Jacob, 1785–1863.
The twelve dancing princesses and other tales from Grimm.
Summary: A collection of fourteen fairy tales by the Brothers Grimm,
including The Donkey, The Mongoose, Iron Hans,
and Jorinda and Joringel.
1. Fairy tales—Germany. [1. Fairy tales. 2. Folklore—Germany.]
I. Grimm, Wilhelm, 1786–1859. II. Lewis, Naomi.
III. Postma, Lidia, ill. IV. Title.
PZ8.G882Gfh 1986 398.2'1'0943 85–6964
ISBN 0–8037–0237–X

Contents

The twelve
dancing princesses

THERE ONCE WAS a king who had twelve daughters, each more
beautiful than the next, who caused him a lot of worry. To ease his fears,
they all slept in the same room, their beds side by side. And every night the
king locked the door and bolted it. Yet every morning when he unlocked the
door he saw that their shoes were worn out from dancing during the night, and
he was unable to discover how this happened. At last, he announced that any
man who found out where the princesses went dancing could choose one of
them for his wife and, what's more, be the next heir to his kingdom. But if a
man came forward, and failed to solve the puzzle within three days and nights,
he would lose his life. And that was that.

It wasn't long before a young prince presented himself to the king, and asked

to try his luck. The king welcomed him heartily, and he was given a room adjoining the great bedroom where the princesses slept. There a couch was made up for him, and the door between the rooms was left unlocked. The prince settled down to his watch, but before long his eyes grew heavy and he fell soundly asleep. When he awoke the next morning, the twelve princesses were fast asleep—but the soles of their shoes were worn through with holes. The same thing happened on the second night and the third.

"Too bad," said the king, and he had the prince beheaded. Many more princes came to try their luck, but each one failed and each one lost his head.

At this time there was a poor soldier who had been wounded many times and was no longer useful to the army. Tramping the roads toward the city he met an old woman who asked what he hoped to find. "I hardly know myself," he laughed. "Perhaps I'll discover where the princesses dance away the night. Why, then I might even get to be king."

The old woman studied him closely. "That's not very hard," she said. "Just don't drink the wine they bring you in the evening, and then pretend to be fast asleep. Here's something else." She handed him a rolled-up cloth. "This is a cloak," she said. "When you put it on you'll be invisible, and you can follow the girls wherever they choose to go."

The soldier had been joking, but the cloak and the good advice made him take the matter seriously. So he gathered up his courage and went before the king. He was greeted warmly, as the others had been. His rags were exchanged for princely clothes, and he was given the same adjoining room. As he was getting ready for bed, the eldest princess brought him a goblet of wine. But the soldier was cunning; he had tied a sponge under his chin and let all the wine run into it so that he didn't taste a drop. Then he lay down, and after a little while he began to snore as though he were soundly asleep.

When the princesses heard him they laughed. "There's another who doesn't value his life!" said the eldest. They began to open cupboards and boxes, and pulled out gowns and jewels. Then they skipped about in their beautiful clothes, prinking before the mirrors. Only the youngest was distracted. "Do you know," she said, "I have a feeling tonight that our luck will run out. Something will go wrong."

"Don't be silly," chided her eldest sister. "You're always worrying. You've seen enough princes come and go to know that there's nothing to fear. Why, this clod would have slept through even without the potion." Still, they looked once more at the soldier. But his eyes were shut tight and his breathing heavy and slow, and they felt safe.

Then the eldest princess went to her bed and tapped on it three times. It sank into the ground, and one by one the princesses disappeared through the opening, the eldest in the lead. Quickly, the soldier threw on his cloak and followed the last and youngest down a flight of stairs. Halfway down he stepped on the edge of her dress, and she stopped in fright. "What's that?" she cried. "Who's pulling at my dress?"

"Don't be a fool," snapped the eldest

9

sister. "You must have caught the hem on a nail."

When they reached the bottom of the stairs, they emerged into a marvelous avenue of trees with silver leaves that sparkled as they moved. I'd better take some proof, the soldier thought to himself, and he reached up and broke off a branch.

The tree let out a terrible roar. "What's that?" cried the youngest princess. "I tell you something is wrong."

"Oh, for heaven's sake," sighed the eldest, "they're just firing a salute at the palace."

Next they came to a magnificent avenue of trees with leaves of gold, and finally to a third whose trees had leaves of glittering diamonds. The soldier broke a branch from each kind of tree, and both times there was such a roar that the youngest jumped and shook with fear even when the sound was gone. But the eldest princess still insisted that all the noises came from gun salutes.

On they walked until they came to a great river. Twelve boats were drawn up to the shore and in each boat sat a handsome young prince. Each of the princesses went to a different boat and climbed on board, the soldier following the youngest. "I don't know why," the prince in the last boat said, "but the boat seems much heavier tonight. It takes all my strength to row."

"Perhaps it is the heat," said the princess. "I feel quite strange myself."

On the other side of the river there was a brightly lit palace and from it lively music could be heard. As soon as they were across, the young couples hurried into the palace, and through the night every prince danced every dance with his own princess. The soldier amused himself by dancing too. And whenever a princess put down her goblet of wine he drained it dry, so that when she picked it up again it was empty. These games made the youngest princess feel more nervous than ever, but the eldest silenced her fears.

They danced until three in the morning, when their shoes were all worn through and they had to stop. The princes rowed them back across the river, and this time the soldier sat in the front boat with the eldest girl. Then, on the bank, the couples said good-bye to each other and the princesses promised to return the following night.

The invisible soldier raced up the stairs, and by the time the sisters came in, slow with exhaustion, he lay on the bed snoring so loudly that they all began to laugh. "We needn't worry about *him*," they said, and after putting away their fine clothes and setting their worn-out shoes under their beds, they lay down and collapsed into sleep.

The soldier decided to say nothing to the king just yet, so he could learn a little more about the strange goings-on. He followed the princesses again on the second and third nights, and everything was the same as before. The third time, the soldier took away a goblet as evidence. When the time came for him to appear before the king, he took with him the goblet, and the silver, gold, and diamond boughs.

The twelve princesses hid behind the door to hear what he would say. "Well," said the king, "have you discovered how my daughters manage to dance through their shoes every night?"

"As a matter of fact," said the soldier, "I have." And he told the king about the twelve princes and the underground palace, and brought out the branches and the goblet to prove his tale.

When the princesses were sent for, they saw there was no use in lying and they admitted everything. Then the king asked the soldier which princess he would like for his wife. "I'm not so young anymore," said the soldier. "I had better have your eldest girl."

The wedding was held that same day, and the king declared that when he died the soldier would inherit his kingdom. As for the twelve princes, the spell they were under was lengthened for exactly as many nights as they had helped the twelve princesses to dance away their shoes.

Cinderella

THE WIFE of a wealthy man fell ill, and when she knew that she was dying she called her only daughter to her bedside. "Dear child," she said, "be good and God will always protect you, and I will look down from heaven and never let you out of my sight." After her mother was buried, the daughter went to her grave every day, and wept, and promised to behave. Then winter came, the snow covered the grave with a white sheet, and when the spring sun drew it off, the man took another wife.

The new wife had two daughters of her own. They were beautiful to look at, but their hearts were as ugly as sin and they hated their stepsister. "Is that stupid creature to sit in the parlor with us?" they asked. "Any lazy girls around here who want to eat will have to earn their food," they told her. "Your place is in the kitchen."

They took the girl's nice clothes away, and gave her only ragged clothing and wooden shoes to wear. "Just look at the princess now, in all her finery," they mocked. Then they pushed her into the kitchen, where she was forced to work from morning till midnight, cooking, scrubbing, carrying wood and water—all the dirtiest chores.

The sisters took special pleasure in plaguing the poor girl. They poured lentils into the ashes and made her pick them out. And at the end of the day, when she was tired out, there was no soft bed for her to lie in but only a heap of ashes by the stove. She looked so dusty and dirty that they called her Cinderella.

One day the father was journeying to another town and he asked his stepdaughters what he should bring them back.

"Beautiful dresses," said one.

"Pearls and jewels," said the other.

"And you, Cinderella," asked the father, "what would you like?"

"Break off the first branch that knocks against your hat on your way home," she said. "Bring that to me."

When the man returned, he had dresses and jewels for his stepdaughters and a hazel twig that had knocked off his hat on the way home for his child. Cinderella thanked him, took the branch and planted it over her mother's grave. Then she cried so much that her tears made it grow. It became a beautiful tree. Every day Cinderella would go and weep and pray beneath it. Every day a small white bird would come to the tree, and whatever the girl wished for the bird would throw down.

Now it happened that the king of the land declared a great celebration, which was to last for three days. All the most beautiful young women of the kingdom were invited, to give the prince an opportunity to choose a wife. The stepsisters were among those asked and they talked of nothing else. When the day arrived, they said to Cinderella, "Hurry up. Fetch our clothes, dress our hair. We are going to the king's palace and we don't want to be late."

Cinderella begged her stepmother to let her go to the grand ball too.

"What, a dirty kitchen maid like you?" said the stepmother. "Why, you haven't so much as a decent pair of shoes. How could you possibly go to the ball?"

But Cinderella still begged to go, and so at last the woman said, "All right, I have emptied a dish of lentils into the ashes. If you have every lentil picked out in two hours you can come to the ball."

Then Cinderella went to the garden and called, "You pigeons, you turtledoves, and all you birds of the sky, come and help me pick

The good into the pot,
The bad into the crop."

At once, two white pigeons flew in through the kitchen window, and after them the turtledoves, and after them, whirring and chirping, all the birds of the sky. They landed among the ashes and began to pick, pick, pick, putting all the good grains into the dish. Before an hour had passed they had finished their task and had flown away.

Cinderella took the dish of lentils to her stepmother. Now, she believed, she would be allowed to go to the ball. But her stepmother thought quickly and said, "How can you go to the palace when you have only rags to wear and can't even dance? You would make us all a laughingstock." Then, when Cinderella began to weep, the stepmother said, "If you can pick two more dishes of lentils out of the ashes within one hour you may come to the ball."

As soon as the woman had emptied the lentils into the ashes, Cinderella slipped into the garden and cried, "You pigeons, you turtledoves, and all you birds of the sky, come and help me pick

The good into the pot,
And you may have what's not."

At once, the two white doves flew in through the window, and then the turtledoves, and then all the birds of the sky. Settling among the ashes, at once they began to pick, pick, pick. In less than half an hour, they had done the sorting and flew away.

Cinderella carried the dishes to her stepmother, thinking that she would be going to the ball. But the stepmother merely said, "You still have nothing to wear, and don't even know how to dance. Do you want to make us look like fools?" And she turned her back on Cinderella, and with her own proud daughters hurried away to the palace.

Left all alone, Cinderella went to her mother's grave and stood beneath the hazel tree. There she said,

"Shake your branches, little tree.
Silver and gold throw over me."

At once, a white bird threw down a gold and silver dress and slippers embroidered with silken silver threads. Cinderella dressed herself in the lovely clothes and hurried to the ball.

So beautiful was she in the sparkling dress that everyone was struck with amazement. She must, they thought, be a princess from some distant land.

The stepmother and sisters thought so too—never dreaming that this was the kitchen girl they had left among the ashes. As for the prince, he took her hand and danced every dance with her, not looking at anyone else.

But at last Cinderella said, "I must go home."

"I will take you there," said the prince, for he wished to know where she lived. But she slipped from his grasp, and though the prince ran after her, she ran ahead and sprang into the pigeon coop. As the prince stood there, wondering, Cinderella's father arrived and asked what had happened to the strange princess. "She leaped into the pigeon coop," said the prince. The father thought it more likely that a girl in the pigeon coop would be Cinderella. Still, he sent for an axe and broke in the wooden door. But the girl had gone.

When the family got home, Cinderella was sound asleep among the ashes, a dim little oil lamp burning on the mantelpiece above. She had jumped from the back of the pigeon coop and run to the hazel tree. There she had left her beautiful clothes and raced back to her place at the hearth.

On the second day of the festival, when the family had left for the palace, Cinderella returned to the hazel tree and said,

"Shake your branches, little tree.
Silver and gold throw over me."

This time the bird threw down an even more marvelous dress, and when Cinderella entered the ballroom, everyone was dazzled by her beauty. The prince had been waiting for her, at once asked her to dance, and would have no other partners all through the evening.

But when it was time for her to go, she again pulled free and ran home and into the garden behind the house. There she scampered, just like a squirrel, into a tree whose boughs were heavy with magnificent pears, and hid herself so well that he couldn't tell where she had gone.

When Cinderella's father arrived, the prince told him, "The strange princess has eluded me again but I think that she is up that tree."

The father thought that a girl in the pear tree would more likely be Cinderella. Still, he sent for an axe and chopped the pear tree down. But whoever was there had gone. When the family returned home, still talking about the beautiful princess who had bewitched the king's son, Cinderella was asleep in the ashes.

On the third day of the celebration, when all the family had gone, Cinderella once again went to her mother's grave, saying,

"Shake your branches, little tree.
Silver and gold throw over me."

And the bird threw down a dress more dazzling than either of the others, and a pair of golden slippers as well. When she entered the ballroom this time, the entire company fell silent, so awed were they by her beauty. The prince again danced only with her and would allow no one else to invite her to dance.

When it was time for her to leave, she slipped from the prince's arms so quickly that he couldn't even follow her. He had, however, foreseen this, and had ordered that the stairs be covered in pitch. As the beautiful maiden fled, one of her golden slippers stuck in the pitch and remained behind.

The next morning, the prince went through the town, the golden slipper in his hand. When he came to Cinderella's father he said, "I am searching for the maiden whose foot fits this slipper. She is the only one I will ever have for my wife."

Hearing this, the stepsisters became excited and begged to try it on. The eldest took the shoe to her room, but it was too small for her foot. So her mother handed her daughter a knife, saying, "Cut off your big toe. When you are queen you won't have to walk anymore."

The greedy daughter cut off her toe, forced her foot into the slipper, and went out to the king's son. True to his word, he asked her to be his bride, and they rode away on his horse. But as they passed the grave of Cinderella's mother, two doves sitting in the hazel tree began to cry,

"Roo-coo, roo-coo,
There's blood within the shoe.
The wrong foot is inside,
Go back for your true bride."

The prince looked down and saw the foot of his bride was streaming blood. He turned his horse around and took the unlucky girl back to her mother. "Let her sister try the shoe," he said.

So the second sister took the slipper into her room, but her feet wouldn't fit in at all. Her mother gave her a knife, saying, "Cut off a bit of your heel. When you are queen you won't have to walk at all."

The daughter did as she was told, forced her foot into the shoe, and limped out to the prince. Once more he thought he had found his bride, and he lifted her onto his horse and rode away. But when they passed the hazel tree, the two doves sitting in its branches cried,

> "Roo-coo, roo-coo,
> There's blood within the shoe.
> The wrong foot is inside,
> Go back for your true bride."

The prince looked down and saw that the foot of his bride was streaming with blood. He turned his horse and took the deceitful maiden back to her mother. "She is not my true bride, either," said the prince. "And yet the slipper has led me here. Have you no other daughter?"

"There is only my first wife's child," said the man. "But she is just a little kitchen drudge and never leaves the house."

"Bring her to me," said the prince.

"Oh, no, my lord," said the stepmother. "The girl is so dirty and squalid, we couldn't possibly allow her in your presence." But he insisted and they had to call her.

Cinderella washed her hands and face, went into the parlor and curtsied to the prince. He handed her the slipper, and she sat on a stool, drew off her heavy wooden shoe, and put on the little golden one. It fitted perfectly. Then he looked at her face and recognized the beautiful maiden who had danced with him, then vanished. "This is my bride," cried the prince.

The stepmother and her daughters went pale with rage. But the prince lifted Cinderella onto his horse and they rode away. As they passed the hazel tree the two pigeons cried,

> "Roo-coo, roo-coo,
> No blood runs from the shoe.
> Happily onward ride,
> For you have your true bride."

Then the birds flew from the tree and landed on the maiden's shoulders, one on the right and the other on the left, and there they stayed.

When the day came for the wedding, the stepsisters went along, hoping at least to share in her good fortune. As the bridal couple went to the church, the elder sister was at the right side and the younger at the left, and as they walked, the doves pecked out one eye from each of them. On the return walk, the elder was at the left and the younger at the right, and the pigeons pecked out the other eye of each. And that was their reward for their falseness and wickedness.

Thousandfurs

THERE ONCE WAS a king whose queen was the most beautiful woman in the world. Her hair was the color of the finest gold, and the king loved her more than life itself. But the queen fell ill, and when she knew that she was dying, she called her husband to her and begged one last favor of him, "Promise me that if ever you marry again, it will be only to a woman as beautiful as I am and with hair as golden as mine." He gave her his word, and she closed her eyes and died.

The seasons came and went, but the king could not be comforted. At last his counselors warned him that his time of mourning must finish and he had to choose a new wife, and he yielded to their advice. Messengers were sent into every corner of the world to find a bride who was as beautiful as his lost queen, but there was no princess in the world whose beauty could match hers, and none who had the same golden hair. So the messengers returned, and the king remained alone.

Now the king had a daughter who was as beautiful as her mother, and she, too, had golden hair. She began to remind the king more and more of his late queen, until one day he looked at her and no longer saw his darling child, but a woman who could take the place of his wife. And he said to his counselors, "If I must marry, I will marry my daughter. She is the very image of her mother, and unless I have her I shall never find a queen."

His counselors were aghast. "Marry your own daughter?" they said to him in horror. "The whole kingdom would suffer from such a sin." But nothing would change his mind. The princess herself was filled with dread. At last, in desperation, she thought of a plan. She said to the king, "Before I consent to marry, I must have three dresses. The first must be as golden as the sun, the second must be as silver as the moon, and the third must be as dazzling as the stars." Since she knew this was impossible, she felt safe.

The king, however, was not to be put off. He had the most brilliant craftsmen in the kingdom weave the three dresses—one as golden as the sun, one as silvery as the moon, and one as dazzling as the stars—and he had them brought to his daughter. "Now you must marry me," he said.

The princess thought quickly. "No," she said. "Before I decide to marry, I must have one more thing—a cloak made of a thousand different kinds of fur, a piece to be taken from every beast in the kingdom."

But again the king was not to be deterred. He sent his finest hunters out to bring a tuft of fur from every creature everywhere in the land. These he had made into a cloak, and he spread it before his daughter, saying, "Our wedding will take place tomorrow."

The princess knew that she must escape immediately, so during the night, when everyone else in the palace was asleep, she gathered together her three most precious things—a golden ring, a golden bobbin, and a little golden spinning wheel. She packed the three marvelous dresses into a nutshell, blackened her hands and face with soot, and wrapped herself in the cloak of a thousand furs. Then, with a silent prayer, she slipped from the palace and set out into the dark.

She walked on through the night, never stopping a moment, until at earliest dawn she crossed the kingdom's border and reached a forest. Tired out, she

crept into a hollow tree and fell asleep. The sun rose high, and still she did not wake.

Now it happened that day that the king of the neighboring land came into the woods to hunt. Suddenly the dogs broke away and began to sniff and bark around the tree where the princess slept. The king stopped and told his huntsmen to see what kind of animal they had found. The men came back looking puzzled. "The creature is like nothing we have ever seen before," they said. "Its coat seems made of a thousand kinds of fur—and it is lying there fast asleep." The king said, "See if you can capture it alive, and we will take it back with us. It may do for future hunting."

As the men drew around her, the princess suddenly woke up in terror, and tried to fight them away. The hunters laughed when they saw that she was a girl, though more like an animal than a human. "It's a wild thing we've got here," they said.

The princess threw herself at their feet. "Take pity on me," she said. "I have no mother or father and I have no home. Please give me shelter." And so they decided to take her back to do dirty work in the kitchen. "At least she won't get any dirtier sweeping up the ashes," they agreed.

So the girl who once had servants was made to fetch wood and water, to stir the fire and pluck the poultry, to dig the herbs and roots and sift the ashes in the kitchen of a strange king's castle. Her sleeping place was a small dark cupboard under the stairs, and here she kept her few belongings. "Ah, wretched princess," she whispered to herself, "whatever will become of you?"

One night, the king held a great ball in the castle. The princess had worked hard, and now she begged the cook to let her creep upstairs and watch for a short while. "I'll hide behind the door," she said. "No one will notice."

"All right," said the cook grudgingly. "But make sure you're back soon."

Quickly the princess ran back to her cupboard, shed her fur covering, washed the soot from her face and hands, and loosened her golden hair. Then she put on the dress as golden as the sun and entered the ballroom.

Struck by her beauty, the guests made way for the stranger. "Who is she?" they asked each other. "Surely she must be the daughter of a king." The king himself came forward and asked her to dance. Never had he seen a woman so lovely, and he vowed to win her heart. But when the dance was over, she was out of his embrace and away so fast that no one knew where she had gone. While the guards were still searching the grounds, the princess was back in her cupboard, pulling off her dress and blackening her face and hands. Soon she was Thousandfurs again, the wild thing of the kitchen. The cook said, "Now that you're back, make the king's soup, while I go up and watch."

So the princess made the soup for the king as the cook had shown her, but when it was done, she added one ingredient of her own—her golden ring. The king was more than pleased with the soup. "It's the best I have ever tasted," he declared. "The cook must be using a new recipe." Then, when he had nearly finished, he saw the gold ring at the bottom of his bowl. "How did this get here?" he asked. "The cook certainly is using some new ingredients. Someone go and bring him to me."

When the cook received the summons, he nearly fainted with fright. "Oh, now what have you done?" he shouted at Thousandfurs. "You must have let a hair fall into the soup or something. It's the end for both of us!"

But the king didn't scold. He simply said, "Tell me who made this soup."

The cook could barely stammer his reply. "I-I-I did, Your Majesty."

"Nonsense," said the king. "It's far too good to have been made by you." And when he learned who had really prepared the dish, he ordered that the wild thing be brought to him.

So Thousandfurs came to the king, her face smudged with soot and ashes. "Just who are you, child?" he asked.

"I'm just a poor homeless girl with no mother or father," she replied.

"What work are you doing here?"

"The only work I'm fit for is to do dirty work and have boots and shoes thrown at my head."

"Do you know where the ring came from that was at the bottom of my soup?" asked the king.

"What ring? I don't know anything about any ring," she answered. The king could get no more out of her, so he let her go back to the kitchen.

Some time later there was another ball at the palace. Once again the princess asked the cook to let her go up for a peek. "All right," said the cook at last. "But make sure that you stay no more than half an hour."

At once the princess ran to her room and washed the soot from her hands and face. This time, however, she put on the dress as silvery as the moon. When she entered the ballroom, everyone stood still, transfixed by her loveliness. The king's heart leaped up, for here was the mysterious vanished maiden, and he hastened to ask her to dance. But as soon as the music stopped, she was gone as before, leaving not a trace behind.

She was—if he had only known—back in the kitchen, her finery gone, preparing his special soup. This time she added the golden bobbin. The moment he tasted the soup, the king knew that the cook could not have made it. And when he discovered the little golden bobbin at the bottom of his bowl, he ordered that the wild girl from the kitchen be fetched before him. But she said that she was only the kitchen maid, and didn't know anything about any golden bobbin, so he had to let her go.

The king decided to give a third ball that year, the finest yet. Again, Thousandfurs asked if she might slip upstairs for a peek. "All right," said the cook, "but don't stay a moment too long."

This time, the princess clothed herself in the dress that sparkled like stars. And this time the king was waiting for her. He signaled to the musicians to make the dance go on longer than usual, and while they were dancing he slipped a gold ring on one of the princess's fingers without her noticing.

When at last the dance was over, she was out of his grasp and ran through the guests as quickly as before. There was no time to change her clothes, so she threw the cloak over the sparkling dress, hastily rubbed some soot on her face, and began to make the soup. In it she dropped the last of her treasures, the golden spinning wheel.

When the king found it in the dish, he sent once again for Thousandfurs, and once again she answered sullenly that she knew nothing about it—she was only the lowest kitchen maid. But she had been too hurried to put soot over her fingers, and the gold ring gleamed against the whiteness of her hand. Before she could disappear, the king put out his own hand and took hers. As she tried to leave, the cloak slipped and he saw the starry dress and the gold of her hair. There she was, the mysterious stranger, the most beautiful maiden ever seen on earth. "You are my dearest bride," he said, "and we shall never part."

The wedding took place, and they lived in the greatest happiness for the rest of their lives.

The donkey

THERE ONCE WERE a king and queen who were rich and handsome and had everything they could want, except a child who would inherit the kingdom.

The queen was very sad and every night she prayed the same prayer, "O grant us a son and heir," she begged, "and we will never be unhappy again."

At last her wish was granted, but not as she had expected. For the newborn prince wasn't a human child at all, but a tiny donkey.

"How could this have happened?" cried the queen, forgetting her pledge of happiness. So great was her disgust that she wanted the servants to drown the little prince, but the king wouldn't hear of it. "He is our son," he said, "and when I die he will be ruler in my place."

The years passed, and in his way the prince grew tall and handsome. He had a gentle, happy disposition, and he was intelligent and a great lover of music. One day he went to the master musician of the palace and said, "Teach me to play the lute as beautifully as you do."

"Ah, dear little master," said the musician cautiously, "you may find that difficult. Your fingers are not the usual shape and they may break the strings."

But the donkey prince would accept no excuse. He was determined to play the lute, and he persevered, practicing at all hours of the day and night, until at last he could play as well as his master.

One day he was out walking and came to a well filled with crystal-clear water. He leaned over the side and saw, reflected back, the head of a donkey, and he knew that it was his own. Now I understand, he thought, why I see no strangers or visitors. Distressed by the discovery, he left the palace, taking only his lute, and went out into the world.

The prince journeyed on, by many roads, until at last he came to a pleasant kingdom ruled by a good old king who had only one child, an extremely beautiful daughter. "I think I'll stop here," he said to himself.

He knocked at the palace gate and called out, "Here's a guest and a stranger! Won't someone let me in?" But no one answered his call. So he took out his lute and began to play so melodiously with his two forefeet that the doorkeeper came to find out who the minstrel was.

When he saw the prince his eyes widened and he ran to the king. "Sire," he said, "outside by the gate is a young donkey playing the lute like a master musician."

"Well, don't leave him out in the cold," said the king. "Bring the musician in so that we all may hear him."

When the donkey-prince came in, however, the courtiers began to laugh, and said that he should be sent to eat with the servants. The prince refused. "I'm no common stable-donkey," he said. "I prefer to sit with the king."

"And so he shall," said the king. "Whoever is a master of his skill is proper royal company."

Then, after the prince had entertained them all with the most beguiling music, the king said, "How does my daughter please you, master lute player?"

"She is the most beautiful damsel I have ever seen," said the donkey.

"Then she shall sit by you," said the king, and they all sat down to eat. His manners were faultless, and everyone was delighted by this unusual guest.

And so the donkey lived in the king's happy court for a long time. But at

length he felt that he ought to move on, for what future had he there? Sadly, he went to the king and asked his permission to go.

"What's wrong?" asked the king. "You look as gloomy as an empty cask of wine. Stay here and I'll give you anything to make you happy. Is it gold you want?"

"No," said the donkey, "I don't want gold."

"Do you want jewels and fine clothes?" asked the king.

"No," said the donkey. "Those things mean nothing to me."

"Would you like half of my kingdom?" asked the king.

"Oh, no," said the donkey, "not even your entire kingdom."

"I wish I knew what would cheer you up, my dear fellow," said the king. "Would you like my daughter as your wife?"

"Yes, I'd like that very much," said the donkey, and all his usual lightness of heart returned.

And so a great and splendid wedding celebration was held. But though the princess was delighted with her unusual bridegroom, the king began to worry

that all might not go well on the wedding night. To allay his fears, he had a servant hidden in the bridal couple's room.

Thinking they were alone, the bridegroom said to the princess, "I will prove to you that I am not unworthy of you."

He threw off his donkey skin, and a wonderfully handsome young prince stood before her. "I never thought that you were unworthy of me," said the princess, "and I could hardly love you more."

When morning came, the prince jumped into his donkey skin, and no one could have guessed what he was like underneath. Soon, the king came to visit his daughter. "Well," he said, "are you happy with your donkey husband?"

"I could not be happier," said the princess. "I love my husband more than anyone in the world."

Then the servant came to the king and told what he had seen. "Don't be ridiculous," said the king. "You must have had too much of the wedding wine."

The man stuck by his story. "Sire," he said, "go tonight and watch for yourself."

That night, when the couple was finally asleep, the king stole into their room and saw in the bed not a donkey, but a remarkably handsome youth. The king snatched the skin from the floor, went out, and had it thrown in the fire, and soon it was nothing but ashes. Then he seated himself outside the couple's door, waiting to see what the young man would do.

The prince woke with the first light of morning and went to put on his donkey skin, but it was not to be found. He was overcome with anguish, "I will be thought an imposter," he said to himself. "My only chance is to escape before anyone else is up."

But when he opened the bedroom door there stood the king. "Where are you off to?" said the king. "Stay here, I beg you; no one wants you to go. Whether as a donkey or a man, you were always a pleasure to have around and as eligible a son-in-law as any king could wish. I am giving you half the kingdom now and the other half when I go."

So the prince stayed, and all were delighted. And when his own royal father died he inherited that kingdom too, and if there was ever a better ruler, we have not heard of him.

The mongoose

THERE ONCE WAS a beautiful princess. But she was vain and proud—not only of her looks, but of her intelligence as well. On the very top of her castle she had a tower with twelve windows all the way around, so from her tower she could see her entire kingdom. But the windows were not made of ordinary glass. From the first one she could see more clearly than usual; from the second still more clearly; from the third even more clearly, and so on to the twelfth, through which she could see everything—whether above or below the surface of the earth. And so there was nothing that was hidden from her, and this gave her immense power.

Willful girl that she was, she had no intention of taking orders from anyone.

Besides, no one she had ever met was anywhere near as clever as she. Any man wanting to marry her had to pass a test, and this was to hide so well that she couldn't find him. Any suitor who failed had his head cut off and mounted on a pole. There were already ninety-seven heads on poles outside the castle, and no suitor had come forward for some time. The princess was delighted. I'll be free for as long as I live, she thought. No man on earth can outwit me.

One day three brothers came to try their luck. The eldest thought he'd be safe if he crept into a deep pit, but the princess saw him from the very first window, and that was the end of *him*. The second thought he'd be safe if he crept into the cellar, but she saw him from the first window too, and his head soon topped the ninety-ninth pole. The youngest brother then asked her to grant him a day's time to think, and also to allow him three tries. Because he was so handsome, and showed more sense than some, the princess said, "As you wish. But you still won't succeed!"

The next day the young man racked his brain to think of a hiding place, but not one idea came. So he took his gun and went out hunting. He was about to shoot a raven when the bird cried, "Don't shoot! I can be of use to you." So the youth lowered his gun, and went on walking until he came to a lake. He was about to kill a large fish when the fish spoke. "Spare me," it cried. "I'll make it worth your while." He let the fish go, and went on walking until he came upon a limping fox. The young man fired, but missed. "You'd do better to come and pull this thorn from my foot," said the fox. He pulled out the thorn, but he still had a mind to kill the little creature for its fur. "Let me go," said the fox. "You won't regret it." So the youth let him go and, as it was getting dark, returned home.

The next day he was supposed to hide, but he didn't know where. At his wits' end, he went to the raven in the forest. "I let you live," he said. "Now show me a hiding place where the princess will never find me."

The raven took an egg from its nest, broke it in half, and put the youth inside. Putting the egg together again, the raven sat on it, and when the princess looked out of the first window, she could find no trace of her suitor. When she couldn't see him through the next window and then the next, she became upset. But when she looked through the eleventh window, there he was—in the raven's nest.

She had the raven shot and the egg brought to her and opened. When the young man was standing before her, she said pleasantly, "If you can't do better than this, you're as good as dead."

So the youth went to the lake the next day and called the fish. "I let you live," he said. "Now show me a hiding place where the princess will never find me."

The fish thought for a while, then said, "The best place is in my stomach." And so he swallowed the young man and swam to the bottom of the lake. The princess looked through her windows—one, two . . . by the time she reached the eleventh and had still not seen him, she was quite disturbed. But when she looked through the twelfth window—there he was, in the stomach of the fish.

She had the fish caught and killed, and the youth cut out. "Well," she said, "only one more chance. The hundredth pole is ready."

On the third day, the youth went into the fields with a heavy heart. At last he found the fox. "You know all about hiding places," he said. "Now show me one where the princess will never find me."

"That's not easy," said the fox. He thought for a while, then cried, "I've got it!" and he led the youth to a spring. There the fox jumped into the water and came out in the form of a peddler. Then the young man dived into the spring and came out as a mongoose.

The peddler took his pretty pet into town. A large crowd gathered around to watch the clever little animal, and at last the princess herself came down. She was so charmed by the little creature that she bought it for a good price. As the peddler handed the mongoose over, he whispered in its ear, "When she goes to the windows, creep quickly under her braids." Then he was gone.

When the next day came, the princess went from the first window to the eleventh without seeing a trace of the young man. Still, she had no doubt that the twelfth would pin him down. But when she looked through the last and saw no sign of him, she was struck with fear and rage and beat at the pane so hard that the glass broke into thousands of pieces.

Stepping back, she suddenly felt the mongoose under her braids. She pulled it out, and in her anger threw it to the ground. It ran outside, where the peddler was waiting, and they hurried back to the spring. When each had returned to his true form, the young man thanked the fox for all his help. "The raven and the fish were clever," he said, "but not as clever as you."

Then he returned to the castle. The princess was waiting, for she knew when she had been beaten.

The wedding was held, and the youth became king—a wise one too—and a good husband. He never told his wife where he had hidden or who had helped him. And soon she stopped asking, for she liked to believe that he had done it by himself and was cleverer than she after all.

Hansel and Gretel

ONCE LONG AGO, at the edge of a great forest, there lived a poor
woodcutter with his wife and two children. The boy was called Hansel,
and the girl Gretel. Times were always hard for them, but then a great famine
seized the land and soon they had almost nothing to eat at all. One night, as he

tossed and turned, unable to sleep, the woodcutter said to his wife, "What is to become of us? How can we feed our children when there is scarcely a crust for ourselves?"

The wife said, "Listen, husband. Tomorrow we will take them deep into the forest. We will light a fire for them and give them each a last piece of bread. Then we will go back to our work. They'll never find their way home again, and we will have a better chance of surviving on our own!"

"I couldn't do that!" cried the poor father. "How can you think of leaving them alone in the woods? Why, they might be torn to pieces!"

"If they stay, we'll all die of hunger," said the wife. "You'd better start getting the coffin-wood now." And she gave him no peace until he stopped arguing, but he still didn't like the idea.

As it happened, Hansel and Gretel had overheard everything that their parents had said. Gretel wept bitterly. "It's the end of us," she said.

"Sh," said the boy, "I'll find a way out, I promise you." And when at last the parents seemed asleep, he crept out of bed, opened the lower half of the door, and went outside. In the bright moonlight the white pebbles all around the house shone like silver coins. The boy stuffed both of his pockets full and went back to his bed.

"Don't worry, Gretel," he said. "God will watch over us. And if he doesn't, I have something else that ought to keep us safe."

At dawn the next morning, the mother shook the children awake. "Get up, you pair of lazybones," she said. "We are going into the forest to fetch wood." She gave them each a small piece of bread. "This is for your dinner," she told them. "But don't eat it too quickly, for there'll be no more today."

The family set out together. But then the father said, "Hansel, why do you keep looking back? You're keeping us waiting."

"Oh, I'm just waving good-bye to my white cat on the roof," said Hansel. "There he is, looking at me."

The woman said, "That's no cat; it's the sun shining on the chimney." But Hansel had really been making a trail of the white pebbles.

At last they came to the dark heart of the forest. "Now children," said the woodcutter, "pile up some wood and I will light a fire to keep you warm."

Hansel and Gretel gathered the wood as their father instructed them. When the little hill of brushwood had been lit, the mother said to them, "Lie down by the fire and rest for a bit. When we've gathered enough wood, we'll come back for you."

The children huddled by the fire, and when midday came they ate their bits of bread. They thought they heard the blows of their father's axe, but the sound came from a branch that he had tied to a withered tree, blowing back and forth in the wind. Tired with waiting, the children fell asleep, and when they awoke it was night.

Gretel began to cry. "How shall we ever find our way home again?" she lamented.

"I told you not to worry," said Hansel. "Just wait until the moon rises, and you'll see." And when the moon was high in the sky, Hansel took his sister by the hand, and following his trail of pebbles, which shined just like silver, he led her home.

It was already dawn when they arrived. When the mother saw them at the door, she said, "You wicked children! Why did you sleep so long? We thought you were never coming!" But the woodcutter rejoiced to see them back.

For a while things went better. Then the famine started again, and the children overheard their mother say to their father, "All we have left is half a loaf of bread. After that, we'd better learn to eat wood. Those two will have to

go. We'll take them farther into the forest this time, and they'd better not try to get back."

The father felt wretched. "I would be happier sharing our last crumbs together," he said. But the woman persisted until he gave in. If you've said yes once, it's hard to say no the next time. And so it was with him.

The children, though, were awake, and heard what was said. Hansel tried to go and gather pebbles as before, but the door was locked; there was no other way to get out. Gretel wept. "Quiet, Gretel," said the boy. "If there's a problem, then there must be an answer too."

Early the next morning, the mother roused the children from their bed. Again she gave them each a piece of bread, but these were smaller than before. Again, Hansel lagged behind the others and, as he walked along, he crumbled bits of bread and made a trail of bread crumbs on the ground.

"Why are you lagging so?" said the father. "What are you looking back for?"

"My little pigeon on the roof is saying good-bye to me," said the boy.

"That's not a pigeon," said the mother, "that's the sun on the chimney." But Hansel went on scattering crumbs until the bread was gone.

Now the woodcutter and his wife led Hansel and Gretel deep, deep into the forest, to a place they had never reached in all their lives before. Then once again the father built them a fire, and the mother said, "Stay here while we are out working, and if you feel tired take a nap. When we are finished, we will come and fetch you."

But hours crept by, and no one came. Gretel shared her piece of bread with Hansel and then they fell asleep. When they awoke it was night.

"Don't worry, Gretel," said the boy. "When the moon rises, we'll be able to follow the trail of crumbs as we did before." But when the moon rose, there were no crumbs to be seen, for the birds had eaten them all.

"Oh, we'll find the way somehow," said Hansel. But they didn't. They walked the whole night and all the next day, and only got themselves deeper into the trees.

By now they were terribly hungry as well as tired, and so they lay down and slept. When they woke up it was their third day in the wood. That afternoon they saw a beautiful, snow-white bird sitting on a bough. It sang so sweetly that they stood and listened. Then it flapped its wings, and flew on ahead of them, as if it wished them to follow. And follow it they did, until it came to a tiny house and settled on the roof.

The house was most unusual. It was made of bread; the roof was of rich iced

cake and the windows of sparkling sugar. "Well," said Hansel, "the Lord must have us in mind. You eat a piece of the window, Gretel. I'll take some of the roof." He reached up and broke off a piece of the roof while Gretel leaned against the window and nibbled at the sweet delicious panes.

And then they heard a soft voice call, from inside:

"Nibble, nibble, mousekin!
Who's nibbling at my housekin?"

The children answered:

"The wind so wild,
The Holy Child,
Nothing more
Is at your door."

But they were too hungry to stop eating. Hansel broke off a good chunk of the roof; Gretel took a whole piece of window pane, and sat on the ground to enjoy it.

Suddenly the door flew open and an old, old woman, hobbled out. The children were so frightened that they dropped the cake and sugar. But the old woman simply said, "Oh, you dear little things, however did you get here? Come inside. There's nothing to be afraid of."

She grasped a hand of each and led them into the house. There she gave them a splendid supper of milk, pancakes, and fruit, and when they could eat no more she tucked them into pretty little beds made with clean white linen. Hansel and Gretel thought they must be in heaven.

But they were wrong. The old woman was not being kind. Oh, no. She was a wicked witch whose favorite dish was roasted child. She had built her wondrous house just to lure them in. Witches, you know, have weak eyesight, but they also have a very keen sense of smell. This witch had known in advance that the two were on the way. "Here's a fine pair," she had told herself. "And they won't get away from me, oh no."

Early the next morning she went to look at them sleeping. "What tasty morsels!" she said. "But they'll do with a bit more fattening." She grabbed Hansel and locked him in a little stone prison with a window barred with iron. "Don't bother to scream," she said. "There's no one here to notice."

Then she poked at Gretel. "Get up, lazy thing," she said. "You must draw some water from the well and start cooking for your brother. I want him nice and fat."

When Gretel saw that her tears had no effect on the witch, she did as she was told. The best of food was now cooked for Hansel, and Gretel got nothing but crab shell. Every morning the witch would hobble over to the shed and cry, "Hansel! Hansel! Stretch out your finger so that I can see how fat you're getting." But clever Hansel always held out a little bone instead.

Why wasn't he getting fatter? thought the witch, whose eyes were too dim to see the truth. But after four weeks, she decided to wait no longer. "Come, you," she called to Gretel. "Go and fetch some water, and no dawdling. I'm going to cook that boy, fat or thin."

Oh, how Gretel wept! "I wish we had died in the forest," she cried. "We'd at least have gone together."

"Oh, stop that blubbing," snapped the witch. And early the next day she told Gretel to light the oven fire while she herself made dough for the pie.

The oven was good and hot. "You get inside," said the witch, "and see if it's right for baking." She had just had the notion that Gretel might make an extra roasted dish. But Gretel guessed what the witch had in mind.

"I don't know how to get in," she said.

"Silly thing," said the witch. "You just creep through; the door is big enough. Look, I can get in myself," and she thrust her head inside to show her.

Quickly, Gretel gave a shove, slammed the door, and the witch was caught within. A foul smoke poured from the chimney along with the witch's screams.

Gretel ran to the stable shouting, "Hansel! Hansel! The witch is dead! We are saved," and opened the door of his prison. They danced about and laughed and kissed until they were all worn out. And then they went all through the

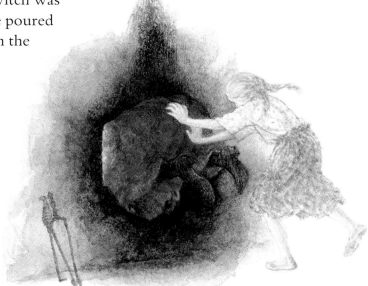

witch's house. Every box and cupboard was filled with precious jewels, and Hansel stuffed his pockets full while Gretel filled her pinafore.

"But now," said Hansel, "we must get out of the forest as quickly as we can."

They walked for several hours and came to a lake. "Not too good," said Hansel, "there's no bridge and no boat."

"But look," said Gretel, "there's a little white duck. I'll ask her if she'll help."

The duck agreed, and Hansel sat on her back. "Come, sit behind," he said to Gretel.

But she said, "No, we would be too heavy. Let her take us one at a time." And the good little duck did that. When they were safely across, they walked on until they reached a part of the forest that seemed familiar, and there they saw, small in the distance, their own house.

At once they both began to run through the woods, up the well-worn path and into their father's arms.

The poor man had never had a happy moment since leaving his children in the wood.

As for the mother, she had died. Hansel and Gretel poured out their jewels all around the room, and they knew that all their cares were over. They all lived in comfort and happiness ever after.

My tale is done.
The mouse can run.
It will make a fur cap if you catch that one!

The spirit in the bottle

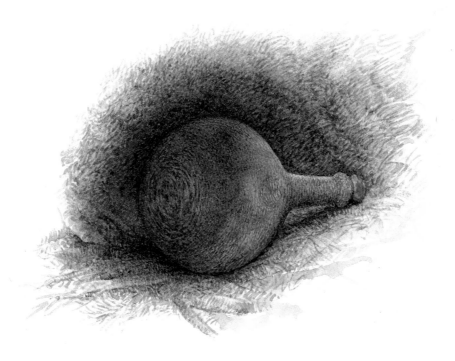

THERE WAS a poor woodcutter who toiled hard for a meager living. But his son was quick and clever, and it was the father's dream that the lad should have a proper education and a real trade, and perhaps be able to take care of him when he grew too old to work. For this he saved every penny he could, until he had enough to send him to college.

The boy did well enough in his studies but, before he had finished, the woodcutter's savings ran out and he had to return home, too educated to be of use with his hands and not educated enough to earn his living with his head.

"It's a shame," said the father sadly, "I don't know what I can do for you now."

But the young student had a good-natured, cheerful disposition. "Don't worry, Father," he said. "Something will turn up—you'll see. Meanwhile, I'll come and help you in the forest."

The father shook his head. "This is no work for you. You will never last out the day. Besides, I have only one axe, and no money to buy another."

But the boy was not to be easily defeated. "Just go to our neighbor and ask him to lend us his axe until I have earned enough to buy one for myself."

So the father borrowed the neighbor's axe, and next morning at daybreak he and his son went into the forest together. The boy worked quickly and well. What's more, he was cheerful company, and his father was well pleased. At last when the sun was directly overhead, he said to the boy, "We will rest a bit now and have our dinner. Then we can continue working as long as the light lasts."

The boy took out his hunk of bread, but he was too lively to sit still. "Take a rest, Father," he said. "I'm going to walk around and look for birds' nests."

"Look for birds' nests?" said the man. "You're a foolish boy. If you don't rest now, you will be so tired later that you won't be able to raise your arm."

"Don't worry about me," said the son mildly. "I'm stronger than you think." And with that he was off. As he walked, he hummed to himself and peered among the leafy branches, looking for birds' nests. At last he came to a huge and ancient oak that five men with outstretched arms could not have spanned. "Plenty of birds must have built their nests up there," he said aloud to himself.

Suddenly he thought he heard a rather muffled voice. It seemed to be crying "Let me out! Let me out!" The boy looked up and down, in back and in front, but he could see nothing. Again the voice called, "Let me out!"

"Where are you?" shouted the student.

"Here in the roots of the oak," came the answer. "Let me out! I beg of you!"

The boy searched among the earth and leaves and at last he found a glass bottle tucked into a hollow. Holding it up to the light, he saw a tiny creature, like a frog, jumping up and down inside. "Let me out!" cried the creature.

So—plop!—the boy pulled out the cork. Instantly the thing slipped from the bottle, growing larger and larger every moment. And there stood a genie, huge and terrible, almost as big as the oak. In a voice that shook the trees the creature roared, "Ha, simpleton! Do you know what your reward is for setting me free?"

"How should I know that?" replied the boy.

"Well, I will tell you," said the spirit with a malicious laugh. "I'm going to break your neck."

"You should have told me that sooner," the boy said calmly. "Anyhow, you can't expect me to take your word for it. We must get a second opinion."

"Never mind your second opinions," mocked the genie. "Why do you think I was shut up in that bottle all those long years? I am the mighty Mercurius. And whoever releases me must die at my hand."

"Just hold on a minute," said the student. "You say you were shut up in that tiny bottle, but it is quite clear from the size of you that you were never inside at all."

"Oh, really!" said the spirit. "I can soon settle that. You watch—I'll show you how it's done." And he drew himself together and poured himself back down the neck of the bottle as quickly as he had leaped out. At once the boy jammed in the cork and pushed the bottle back among the roots.

He was just about to leave when the spirit cried out pitifully, "Please let me out! I beg you, let me out!"

"Oh, no," said the student. "You can't play that trick twice."

"If you set me free," persisted the spirit, "I vow that you will have everything you want for the rest of your life."

"If I set you free," said the boy, "you will cheat me a second time."

"I swear to you," cried the spirit, "that if you let me out, I'll do you no harm, and I'll reward you beyond your dreams. Why don't you take a chance?"

Well, thought the boy, he has a point there. Maybe he means it, and, if not, I'm prepared. He won't get the better of me. So once again he pulled the cork from the bottle, and the genie rose up and up as he had done before. He stretched himself happily, looked down, and handed the student a piece of cloth that looked just like a bandage. "Here's your reward," he said. "If you put one end of this cloth over a wound, the wound will heal immediately. And if you rub steel or iron with the other end, it will change to silver."

"Wait until I have tested it," said the boy. He took his axe and made a gash in a tree. Then he touched the wound with one end of the cloth, and at once it closed together and was healed.

"Now we can part," said the boy. "It's a good reward, and I thank you."

"I thank you too," said the spirit, and was instantly gone.

"Where have you been all this time?" asked the worried father when his son returned. "We still have hours of work to do."

"Don't worry, Father," said the boy cheerfully. "I'll soon make up for lost time. Watch! I'm going to split that tree in two."

Quickly he rubbed his axe with the cloth and dealt the tree a blow. But, as the iron had turned into silver, the blade simply bent.

"Oh, Father," teased the boy. "Look what a cheap axe you have given me. One good blow and it bends."

The poor man was beside himself with worry. "Now look what you've done!" he shouted. "Where will I get the money to pay for a new one? You students have no idea of what the real world is like."

For a while they sat in silence. Then the boy said, "Father, since the axe won't work, why don't we take the rest of the day as a holiday?"

The woodcutter was horrified, "Holiday? You can take a holiday if you want, but I must keep on working if we're going to keep on eating. You go home and I'll be back later."

"Very well, Father," said the boy. "But this is my first time in the woods. You must show me the way."

The father's anger had died down and left him spent, so he agreed to turn back early. "But before you do anything else," he said, "take that axe to the blacksmith and see what he'll give you for it. Even a few pennies will help."

The boy agreed. But he went not to the blacksmith, but to the silversmith. The man tested the silver axe and laid it on the scales. "It's worth four hundred ducats," he said, "but I don't have that much money on me."

"Give me what you have, and you can owe me the rest," said the boy. The silversmith gave him three hundred ducats and the boy went back to his father.

"I've sold the axe," he said. "Go and ask our neighbor how much he wants."

"I know that already," replied the old man. "Two ducats."

"Then give him twice as much," said the boy. "Look!" And he thrust a handful of gold coins into his father's hand. "From now on you can have all you want."

"But how have you come by all this money?" said the father. "What have you done?"

Then the son described his adventure with the genie. "Didn't you know," he ended, "that if you're ready to take chances, everything will be all right in the end?"

Now the boy could afford to go back to college and finish his studies. And with the help of the magic cloth that could heal all wounds, he became the most famous doctor in the world.

One-eye, Two-eyes, and Three-eyes

THERE WAS ONCE a woman who had three daughters. The eldest was
called One-eye, because she had only one eye in the middle of her
forehead; the second was called Two-eyes, because she had two eyes like
ordinary people; and the third was called Three-eyes, because she had three
eyes, one at each side and one in the middle of her forehead. The woman and
her two misformed daughters hated Two-eyes. "You are so common," they
said. "You look just like other people. You are not one of us!" They treated her
like a slave, giving her only their worn-out rags to wear and leftover scraps to
eat, and they made her do all the dirtiest chores.

One day Two-eyes was out in the fields, looking after the goat. Miserable
with hunger, she sat down on a grassy bank and began to weep. Her tears ran
down and down.

Then she heard a voice say, "Why are you crying, Two-eyes?"

Looking up, she saw a woman standing near. "I have good reason to cry,"
said the girl. "My mother and sisters hate me because I have two eyes like
ordinary people. They give me nothing to wear but cast-off rags and nothing
to eat but scraps. Today they gave me so little food that I feel faint and
starving."

"Wipe away your tears," said the woman, "and I will tell you something that will keep you from ever being hungry again. You must say these words to your goat:

> Little goat, whom I tend,
> I pray you send,
> Little friend,
> What will make my hunger end.

"A table will appear set out with all kinds of delicious food. When you have eaten your fill, just say:

> Little goat, you served me well.
> Now use again your magic spell,
> That where the feast was, none can tell."

Having said those words, she was gone. Two-eyes decided to try the charm straight away.

> "Little goat, whom I tend,
> I pray you send,
> Little friend,
> What will make my hunger end."

Scarcely had she spoken than a little table was standing before her. It was covered with a fresh white cloth, and a place was set with a knife and fork and a silver spoon. Heaped on it was a choice of the most delicious foods, with savory cooked dishes all hot and steaming, as though they had just come from the stove. Two-eyes said the shortest prayer she knew—"Lord God, be with us always. Amen"—and helped herself to some of each kind of food. When she could eat no more, she repeated the second charm that the woman had taught her:

> "Little goat, you served me well.
> Now use again your magic spell,
> That where the feast was, none can tell."

Immediately the table and everything on it vanished into thin air.

When she got home she found her scraps of supper on a coarse earthenware plate, but she left them where they were. The next day she again went out with the goat, but she didn't touch the miserable stale bread put out for her dinner.

The first few times she did this, her sisters said nothing, but when it happened every day, they grew suspicious and said to their mother, "There's something very odd going on. She used to be grateful for any crumb we gave her, but now she doesn't even look at it. She must have found some other way of getting food."

In order to learn the truth, the mother resolved to send One-eye along with Two-eyes when she next went to drive her goat to the pasture. So when Two-eyes was getting ready to set out, One-eye said to her, "I am going with you today to see that the goat is properly fed and looked after."

Two-eyes, however, knew her sister well and guessed what was in her mind. She made her walk far afield, driving the goat into high grass, and at last she said, "Come, One-eye, we can rest here for a while and I will sing you a song."

Exhausted by walking and the heat of the midday sun, One-eye sat down, growing more and more drowsy, while Two-eyes sang, "One-eye, are you waking? One-eye, are you sleeping?" over and over and over again. At last One-eye shut her eye, and fell sound asleep.

As soon as she saw this, Two-eyes repeated the woman's magical words. At once, the table of good things appeared, and Two-eyes sat down to eat. When she was done, she recited the second charm, and everything neatly vanished. Then Two-eyes shook her sister awake. "One-eye," she said, "you can't take care of the goat and go to sleep at the same time. It might run anywhere! Get up, it's time to go home again."

Home they went, and again that night Two-eyes didn't touch her meager plate of food. "Now, One-eye," said the mother, "what did you find out? Why isn't she hungry at night?"

"I don't know," said the girl. "I saw nothing. But I did fall asleep for a while in the meadow."

The next day, the mother sent Three-eyes out to keep watch. But Two-eyes guessed what she had in mind, and drove the goat far afield and into the highest grass. At last she said, "We'll stop here and rest awhile, and I'll sing you a song."

Three-eyes, exhausted with the walking and the heat of the midday sun, was all too ready to sit down and soon became drowsy. Two-eyes began to sing the same song as before, but her thoughts wandered, and instead of singing, "Three-eyes are you waking? Three-eyes are you sleeping?" she carelessly sang, "Three-eyes are you waking? Two-eyes are you sleeping?" Two of her sister's eyes shut tightly in sleep, but the third had not been named in the song, and it stayed alert even though the cunning Three-eyes pretended to close it too.

When Two-eyes thought that her sister was fast asleep, she repeated the charm and caused the table to rise once again. She ate and drank as much as she wished, and said the second verse, causing the table to vanish again. But Three-eyes had seen everything with her one unsleeping eye.

Presently Two-eyes shook her sister, saying, "Is this how you take care of the goat? Get up, it is time to go home."

As soon as they were back, Three-eyes said to the mother, "I have discovered why Miss High-and-Mighty won't touch our food anymore." And then she told her all about the song and the table and the fabulous assortment of food, and the song by which Two-eyes had tried to put her to sleep.

"What's this!" the woman cried. "She may think she's got the better of me, but she'll soon find out she's wrong." Then, taking up a butcher's knife, she went into the yard, thrust it into the heart of the goat, and it fell dead.

Two-eyes was overwhelmed with grief. She ran out into the fields and sat once more on the grassy bank, weeping bitter tears. Suddenly she saw the wise woman, standing, looking down.

"Why are you crying now?" the woman asked.

"I have good reason to cry," said the girl. "My mother has killed the little goat. Your charm is of no more use, and I must go back to my life of hunger and want."

The woman said, "Listen to me, when you go home, ask your sisters to give you the entrails of the goat, and bury them in the ground in front of your house. Do this, and your luck will change, I promise you." With those words, she vanished.

Two-eyes went home and begged her sisters for a piece of the slaughtered goat. "I don't ask for the good parts," she said, "just the entrails."

Laughing, they threw her the entrails, saying, "These are good enough for the likes of you." Two-eyes thanked them, then cautiously buried them as the woman had told her, just outside the house.

When they awoke the next morning, there in front of the cottage stood a marvelous tree, with leaves of silver and fruit of the brightest gold—the most beautiful tree that you could ever imagine. They wondered how it could have grown from their soil, but Two-eyes knew that it rose from the spot where she had buried the entrails of the goat.

Then the mother said to her eldest daughter, "Climb up the tree, my girl, and bring us some of the fruit."

One-eye climbed up into the tree, but every time she stretched out her hand for one of the golden apples, the branch jumped from her hand.

"Never mind," said the mother. "Come down. Three-eyes can see more; she'll go up and fetch some fruit."

Three-eyes took her sister's place, but she had no better luck. Furious with impatience, the mother herself climbed up into the tree, but every time she reached for an apple she found herself clutching empty air.

"Would you like me to try?" asked Two-eyes.

Her sisters hooted with scornful laughter. "You, with your common two eyes, what can you hope to do that we haven't done?"

But Two-eyes climbed up, and the golden apples did not bob from her grasp but moved into her hand of their own accord. Soon her apron was full of the lovely fruit. Her mother and sisters quickly took it from her, but so great was their envy at her success that from then on they treated her even more cruelly than before.

One day they were all standing near the tree when a young knight came riding by. "Quick, Two-eyes," the sisters cried, "hide yourself under this barrel so that you don't disgrace us with your ugliness." Hastily, they turned the barrel over the girl and pushed in the golden fruit she had been gathering.

The handsome young lord stopped his horse and admired the magnificent tree. "I have never seen anything so beautiful in all my life," he said with wonder. "Who owns this marvel? I would give anything to have just one branch of it for my own."

"The tree is ours," said One-eye and Three-eyes promptly. "We'll certainly get you a branch.' But no matter how hard they tried, both branches and fruit moved from their reach every time.

"It seems strange," said the knight, "that this should be your tree and yet you cannot even touch the boughs."

"Of course it's ours," said the sisters angrily. "Whose else would it be?" But Two-eyes was so indignant at their lies that she rolled a golden apple from beneath the barrel, and it stopped at the young man's feet.

"What's this?" he asked.

The sisters then told him that they had another sister, too common to be allowed to show herself by the light of day. "She has two eyes, the ugly thing," they explained.

"I'd like to see her, though," said the knight.

So Two-eyes lifted the barrel and came out. The young lord was amazed at her beauty. "Two-eyes," he said, "I think that you will be able to break off a branch from this tree for me."

"Indeed, I can," said Two-eyes, "for the tree is mine." She climbed up nimbly and with the greatest ease broke off a branch of silver leaves and golden fruit, and handed it to the knight.

He said to her, "What can I give you for this precious gift?"

Two-eyes answered, "While I am here, I suffer from hunger and thirst, from grief and want, from morning until night. If only you would take me away and save me from this misery, I would ask no more."

At once, the young lord lifted her on his horse and took her home with him to his father's castle. He loved her so much that they were married without delay, and the wedding was held with great rejoicing everywhere.

As they watched their sister ride away with the handsome knight, the sisters consoled themselves with the fact that they still, at least, had the wonderful tree. "Even if we can't get the fruit," they said, "people will stop and admire, and we may have even better luck than that girl." But the next morning when they looked out, the tree had vanished, and all their hopes with it. And when Two-eyes looked out of her castle window that same morning, there was the tree below. It had chosen to follow her.

One day two poor women came to the castle, begging for alms. When Two-eyes looked at them closely, she recognized her own sisters, so cast down by poverty and ill-luck that they were forced to wander from door to door, begging for their bread. Moved by their plight, she made them welcome and looked after them with kindness, and they truly repented of the evil they had done her in their youth.

Iron Hans

THERE WAS ONCE a mighty king who owned a great forest filled with all kinds of wild animals. One day he sent out a huntsman to shoot him a roe, but the man did not return. "Maybe something has happened to him," said the king. So he sent out two more huntsmen to find the first, but they, too, never returned. On the third day the king sent forth all his remaining hunters, saying, "You are not to come back until you have found the missing men." But they, too, were never seen again. And so for many a year no one in the kingdom would step so much as a foot into the treacherous woods.

Then one day a strange huntsman came to the king seeking work, and offered to go into the forest to prove his skill. The king shook his head. "No, no, you would fare no better than the others."

The man replied, "Sire, I do this at my own risk." He called his dog, and they entered the haunted forest.

After a short while, the dog took off after some game, but had to halt at the edge of a deep pool. At once an arm rose out of the water, seized the dog, and drew it down below. Seeing this, the hunter went back to the castle and fetched three men with buckets. They baled out all the water—and there at the bottom lay a wild man whose body was the color of rusty iron and whose hair hung down to his knees. They bound the creature with chains and brought him back to the castle, where the king had him put in an iron cage in the courtyard. No one was to open the cage on pain of death, and the queen herself was given charge of the key.

The king had a little son who liked to play in the courtyard. One day his golden ball fell into the prisoner's cage. "Throw me out my ball," called the prince.

"Not until you open this door for me," answered the wild man.

"But I can't do that," answered the boy. "My father has forbidden it."

The next day he again asked the wild man for his ball.

"First open my door," said the man.

"I dare not," pleaded the boy, but he still longed for his ball.

On the third day, when his father was out hunting, he again returned to the cage. "I couldn't open the door even if I wanted to," he said. "I don't have the key."

"The key is under your mother's pillow," answered the wild man.

The young prince cast caution to the winds and fetched the key. But the lock was stiff and rusty and, in freeing the man, the boy hurt his finger.

The wild man stepped out, handed the prince his golden ball, and began to hurry away. The boy became afraid and cried out to him, "Oh, wild man, don't go away or they'll beat me." The man turned back, set the boy on his shoulders, and with long swift strides made for his home in the woods.

The first sight that greeted the king on his return was the empty cage. "What's been happening here?" he roared at the queen.

"Nothing that I know of," she replied. But when she went to get the key, she found that it was gone. So, too, was her little son. The king sent his men to search high and low for the prince, but no trace of him was ever found, and the king and queen and their court were filled with grief.

Once in the forest, the wild man set down the boy. "You will never see your parents again," he said, "but I will look after you. You showed me kindness and deserve the same from me. If you do all I tell you, you will fare well, for I have more riches than anyone else in the world." Then he made the child a bed of moss, and told him to go to sleep.

The next morning, he took the prince far into the woods, until they came to a spring. "You see how clear and bright this is," said the wild man. "I want you to see that nothing falls in to spoil it. I will come back in the evening."

The boy sat by the spring and watched. Sometimes he saw a golden fish or a golden snake dart through the water, but he took care to let nothing fall in. After a while his injured finger began to ache, and without thinking, he dipped it in the cool stream. Remembering instantly, he drew it out, but already it was covered with gold which no amount of rubbing could remove.

In the evening the man returned. "What has happened to the spring?" he asked.

"Nothing," said the prince, hiding his finger behind his back.

But the wild man was not fooled. "You've dipped your finger into the water," he said. "I will let it pass this time, but make sure that it doesn't happen again."

Early the next day, the boy went on guard as before, but in spite of all his vigilance a hair from his head drifted into the water. At once he fished it out, but it had turned to gold.

When the wild man returned in the evening, he knew immediately what had happened. "You have let a hair fall in the spring," he said. "I will let it pass this time, but if anything else touches the water, it will all be polluted—and you will have to leave me for good."

On the third day, the prince once more took up his post. But the hours were long and tedious, and at last to amuse himself he began to stare at his own reflection mirrored in the spring. He became so engrossed that his long hair tumbled over and, to his horror, it reached the water. He sat up quickly, but every hair on his head had turned to gold. It looked bright as the sun.

Terrified, the poor boy tried to cover his shining hair with a handkerchief, but the wild man could not be deceived. "Untie that handkerchief," he said. The boy's golden hair spilled out.

"You have failed the test," said the wild man sadly, "and can no longer stay with me. You must go into the world and learn what life is all about. But because you have a good heart and I wish you well, I will grant you a favor. If you are ever in need of help, come to the forest and call 'Iron Hans!' three times."

Then the king's son journeyed long and far until he reached a great city. There he looked for work, but as he had never been trained for anything, there was no work to be found. At last he went to the palace and begged to be taken in. "I'm quick to learn and I'll work hard," he said. So he was given a place in the kitchen, doing the dirty work.

One day when there was no one else on hand, the cook ordered the boy to take the king his dinner. But to keep his golden hair well hidden, the prince always wore a cap. So when he went to the royal table, the king said, "Tut, tut, tut, boy, don't you know that you mustn't wear that thing in the royal presence?"

"Your majesty," pleaded the boy, "I cannot remove my cap, because I have a terribly sore head."

The king called the cook before him and scolded him soundly for taking such a boy into his service. "Send him away at once," he ordered. But the cook liked the boy and exchanged him for the gardener's apprentice.

The prince had to work very hard in the garden, planting and watering, hoeing and digging. One summer day when he was alone, he felt so hot that he

took off his cap to cool his head in the breeze. So dazzling was his golden hair that the king's daughter noticed it from her window.

"Boy," she cried. "You there, bring me a bunch of flowers."

Hastily the prince put his cap back on and gathered some wild field flowers for the princess. Then he took the bunch to her room.

"Take off your cap," she said. "It isn't right for you to keep it on in my presence."

"I can't," said the boy. "I have a sore head."

The princess simply put out her hand and plucked the cap from his head. His golden hair fell down his shoulders—truly a wonderful sight. He tried to run away, but she caught his arm and gave him a handful of gold coins. He took them, but since he cared nothing for money, he gave them to the gardener's children.

The next day, the king's daughter again called to him to bring her a fresh bunch of flowers. Once more she snatched at his cap, but he was ready for her this time and held it fast with both hands. So she let him go— with another handful of coins, and again he passed them on to the gardener's children. On the third day, the same scene was acted out. She could not get his cap; he would not keep her money.

Sometime later, a horrible war overran the country. The king gathered together all his troops, but he doubted their strength against the powerful enemy. The gardener's boy said to the soldiers, "I'll go with you to the war, if only someone will give me a horse."

The others laughed at him. "We will leave one behind in the stable for you," they said.

When they had gone, the prince went into the stable to find his horse. It was so old and lame that it could scarcely manage to walk.

Still, he mounted it and went off slowly to the forest. There he stopped and called out "Iron Hans" three times.

The wild man promptly appeared. "What is it you want?" he asked.

"I want a strong steed, for I am going to the war."

"You shall have your steed," said the wild man. "That and more." He vanished into the forest and immediately a groom appeared, leading a magnificent horse, while behind him followed a great troop of soldiers. The prince leaped on the mighty stallion, and rode out at the head of the soldiers.

When they neared the battlefield, they found the king's forces only minutes away from a terrible defeat. The prince and his men rushed into the thick of the battle. The enemy began to flee, but the young man and his troops gave chase and never stopped until there was not a single invader left in the land. Instead of returning to the king, however, the prince led his men back to the forest and called for Iron Hans.

"What is it you want now?" said the wild man.

"All I want is for you to take back your horse and your army and give me back my lame old nag."

And that was how he returned. The others laughed to see him. "What a soldier!" they mocked. "You never even made it to the battle."

The princess was waiting to meet her father when he returned in triumph. "You have had a great victory," she cried.

"Ah," sighed the king. "I am not really the victor. We would have lost if a strange knight had not appeared with his soldiers and routed the enemy."

"Who was he?" asked the princess. But the king said, "I know nothing of him. He came out of nowhere, and that's where he disappeared to."

Then he proclaimed celebrations that were to last for three whole days. "On each day you will throw a golden apple to the knights," said the king. "Perhaps our unknown hero will appear."

When the celebrations were announced, the prince went back to the forest and called for Iron Hans. "What is it that you want now?" the wild man asked.

"I just want to catch the princess's golden apple," said the prince.

The wild man smiled. "It's as good as yours already. But you must look the part. I'll give you a suit of red armor and a chestnut mare."

So on the first day of the feast, the prince galloped into the courtyard and took his place among the other knights. When the princess came forward and threw a golden apple to the assembled men, he caught it easily. At once he galloped away and was gone.

On the second day of the feast, Iron Hans gave him white armor and a magnificent white horse. Again he caught the apple, and again he was gone like the wind. The king was furious. "If it happens a third time, I want him pursued and caught," he stormed.

For the third day of the feast, Iron Hans sent the young man off in black, riding a great black stallion. Once again the prince caught the apple and sped away; but this time the king's men gave chase, and one got near enough to wound him with his sword. The prince still escaped, but his helmet fell to the ground and his golden hair blew freely in the wind. Amazed, the men gave up their pursuit and returned to tell the king what they had seen.

When the princess heard of the knight's brilliant hair, she went to the gardener to ask him about his boy. "He's an odd one," said the gardener. "The children say he showed them some golden apples he won, but he is always filling their heads with nonsense."

Then the princess told her father to send for the gardener's boy. The boy still wore his cap, but the princess quickly took it from his head. Now everyone could see his golden hair, and all were struck with wonder at his looks.

"Are you the knight who came to the festival each day and caught the three golden apples?" asked the king.

"I am," said the boy. "And here are the apples, which I return to you." He took them from his pocket and handed them to the king. "I am also the knight who helped you to beat your enemy in battle."

"If you can do such deeds," said the king, "you are the most remarkable gardener's boy I've ever seen. Who are you truly? What can I give you?"

"My father is himself a mighty king," said the prince, "and I have all the gold that I will ever need."

"Is there any reward that you will accept?" asked the king.

"There is," said the prince. "I would like your daughter for my wife."

The princess was delighted. "I *knew* he was no gardener's boy," she said.

There was a great and joyful wedding for the royal couple. Happiest of all the guests were the prince's parents, who had long abandoned hope of seeing their son again. In the midst of the wedding feast the doors suddenly opened as though blown by a strong wind. Then a proud king with a mighty retinue entered. He strode up to the bridegroom and embraced him heartily.

"I am Iron Hans," he said. "I was turned into a wild man by an evil spell, but you have set me free. You are my sole heir, and everything I own will come to you."

The Nixie of the mill pond

THERE WAS ONCE a miller who lived with his wife in perfect happiness. Work was plentiful; they had money and land, and the mill did better each year. But bad luck can come suddenly, and so it happened to the miller and his wife. Their money began to dwindle, their land was lost, and soon they couldn't even call the mill in which they lived their own.

And now the man was so weighed down with care that his days were wretched, and in the nights he tossed and turned, never able to rest. At last, one dawn, weary of trying to sleep, he rose from his bed and went to walk outside.

As he neared the mill dam, and the first rays of sun lit the sky, he heard a sudden rippling in the pond. Turning around, he saw a beautiful young woman rise slowly from the water, her long hair falling down in silken streams, covering the pale whiteness of her body.

At once he knew that this was the Nixie of the mill pond, and he stood rooted to the spot with fear. But she said to him very quietly, "Good miller, why are you so sad?"

Beguiled by the sweetness of her voice, he began to tell her of his troubles. "I am at my wits' end," said the poor man. "Everything is gone."

"Don't upset yourself," said the Nixie. "If you but promise me one thing, I will make you richer than ever you were before."

"And what is that one thing?" said the miller.

"You must promise me the first thing you find born in your house when you return."

What could that be but a little cat, or dog, or mouse? thought the miller. "All right," said he. "It's a bargain." The Nixie vanished into the water, and the miller turned for home.

He was puzzled to see the serving girl waiting at the door. "Master!" she called out. "Come! Your wife has just given birth to a fine baby boy."

The miller was struck with horror at the Nixie's guile, and went in with dragging steps. "Why do you look so sad?" said the wife. "You should rejoice."

So he told her what had happened, and they agreed that the child must never go near the pond. "If you do," they used to tell the boy, "the water spirit will seize you and drag you down." Still, the Nixie kept her word: the mill worked busily once again and all the debts were paid. Often they forgot the pact.

The boy grew up, and in time was apprenticed to a huntsman. When he learned all that he could, the lord of the village took him into his service. Presently the young man fell in love with a village maiden who was as beautiful as she was good, and when the young couple decided to be married, the lord gave them a house, with his blessing. And they lived in peace and happiness.

One day the young hunter was in the woods when he spied the finest roe he had ever seen. He at once gave chase, but the roe eluded him, always keeping slightly out of range. At last it ran into open country, and the hunter was able to shoot it dead. He had been so engrossed in the chase, however, that he had failed to notice that he was near the dangerous mill pond, and after he had disemboweled the deer, he automatically went to the water to wash his blood-

stained hands. Scarcely had he dipped them in than the Nixie rose up laughing from the depths. She wound her white cold arms around him and drew him into the pond.

When evening came and the hunter did not return, his young wife became alarmed. At last she went out to look for him, but she could find no trace at all. Then she remembered the threat that hung over him, and hurried to the forbidden pond. There she found his hunting pouch, still lying on the bank, and she knew too well what had happened.

Weeping and wringing her hands, she called out her husband's name, but nothing broke the silence. For hours she paced up and down like a mad woman, now cursing the Nixie, now pleading with her for her husband's return. But no sign or sound ever came from the pond, and the surface stayed quite still, reflecting only the crescent of the moon.

At last the poor wife's demented strength came to an end, and she collapsed onto the ground and slept. In her sleep she dreamed that she was climbing up a steep rocky mountain. Thorns and briars caught at her feet; the wind whipped her hair about her face; she was stung by rain and hail. But she struggled on until she reached the summit. There all was different; the sky was blue, the breeze was warm and gentle, and before her, in a green and flowering meadow, stood a tiny cottage. She went up to the cottage and opened the door, and there sat an old white-haired woman who smiled at her kindly, beckoning her to come in. But just as she was about to speak to the woman, the young wife woke.

Night was over; the sky was light with dawn. So vivid was her dream,

however, that she determined to act on it. And so she set out to climb the mountain. The thorns tore at her flesh, the stinging hail lashed her face, and the wind tried to prise her from her perilous hold. But at last she reached the top, and there, as in her dream, were the blue skies and the green field and the pretty little cottage. When she opened the door, the old woman smiled and asked her to sit down. "You must be in trouble," she said, "if you have sought me out in this lonely cottage."

Weeping, the young wife told her story. "Don't cry," said the wise old woman when the story was at an end. "I will help you get your husband back again. Here is a golden comb. When the full moon has risen, go to the mill pond, sit on the shore, and comb your long black hair. Then lay the comb on the bank and pretend to sleep. But watch to see what happens."

"O thank you, thank you, mother," said the wife, and left for home.

At the next full moon the young woman hurried to the mill pond, sat down on the bank, and combed her long black hair with the golden comb. When she was done, she placed the comb at the water's edge and lay as if asleep. Quite soon there was a movement in the water's depths, and a wave rose up and clawed out to the shore, bearing the comb away. Then the surface parted and the head of the hunter rose from it. He uttered not a word, but looked at his wife with a piercing sadness. And then a second wave rose over him and drew him down once more. A moment later the pond lay perfectly still, with nothing to be seen in it but the shining face of the moon.

Her sorrow renewed, the young wife returned to her empty home. That night she dreamed again of the cottage and the old woman, so the next

morning she set out to see her once more. This time the woman gave her a golden flute. "Wait until the full moon comes again," she instructed her. "Go to the pond, play the prettiest tune you know on this flute. After that, lay the flute on the bank of the pond, pretend to sleep, and watch what happens."

The young wife did exactly as the old woman had told her, and when the full moon rose again she sat by the mill pond and played the most moving tune she knew. Then she carefully laid the flute at the edge of the water. Immediately, there was a swirling in the water's depths, and a wave rose up and took the flute away. And then the water parted and her husband appeared, half his body rising out of the pool. He stretched his arms out to her with longing, but at once a second wave came up and drew him down.

"What good does it do me," cried the unhappy wife, "to see my beloved, only to lose him again?" But that night she dreamed for a third time of the tiny cottage and the wise old woman. And for a third time she toiled to the top of the mountain.

This time the old woman gave her a golden spinning wheel. "All is not yet fulfilled," she said. "Wait again until the moon is full, then sit yourself on the bank of the pond with this spinning wheel. Spin until the spool is full, then leave the wheel near the water, as you have done before. After that—you will see what you will see."

Again the wife did what she was told. As soon as the moon was full, she carried the golden spinning wheel to the pond, and there she sat and spun until the spool was filled with thread. Then she placed the wheel on the bank and at

once a mighty wave rose up and bore it away. Just as quickly, the hunter appeared in a great spout of water.

Springing to the shore, he caught his wife by the hand and they fled together, but they had covered only a few paces when they heard a terrible roaring. The pond had left its place, and raged toward them over the open country.

The lovers felt that their end had truly come, and with the last of her strength the wife cried out, "Old woman, old woman, I beg you to help us now." In an instant, they were miraculously transformed; she into a toad, and he into a frog. Now the flood could not destroy them, but it did tear them apart and carry them far, far away.

When the water had receded and they touched dry land again, the young man and his wife returned to their human forms. But each had no idea where the other was. Nor did they know the land in which they had surfaced. High mountains and deep valleys lay between them and kept them from each other and from their home.

In the lonely years that followed, they made their livings by tending sheep. One spring, when the earth was soft and green again, and the sun was warm and bright, they both went out with their flocks to find fresh pastures and came, by chance, to the same valley.

At first they did not recognize one another. Yet, they felt a curious pleasure in each other's company, and after that first meeting returned each day with their sheep to this green place. One evening when the moon was full and the flocks had settled to rest, the shepherd pulled the golden flute from his pocket and began to play a sad but beautiful tune. When his song was finished, he saw that the shepherdess was weeping.

"Why are you crying?" he asked.

"I cry," she said, "because the last time I played that tune on the flute, I saw my husband rising from the pond where he was held by a water spirit."

He looked at her, and she looked at him, and it seemed as though a veil had been drawn from their eyes.

"It is you!" cried the shepherd.

"It is you!" said she.

They hugged and kissed, and all the unhappiness of the past years vanished forever.

Jorinda and Joringel

THERE ONCE WAS a castle in the heart of a great forest, and in the castle lived a wicked witch. During the day she went around in the form of a cat or a screech owl, but at night, when evil could walk freely, she took on human shape. If any man came within a hundred paces of her home, she amused herself by making him freeze like stone exactly where he stood, until she broke the spell. But if the intruder was a girl, she turned her into a bird and shut her up in a wicker cage. Behind those walls were over seven thousand wicker cages, and in each was a beautiful bird who had once been a human maiden.

Now in the village bordering the forest lived a beautiful young girl named Jorinda. She was engaged to marry Joringel, a youth who was good and handsome, and they longed to be always together.

One day toward sundown they went out walking, and wandered hand in hand into the forest. "We must take care," said Joringel, "or we'll find ourselves too close to the witch's castle." It was an evening of unearthly beauty. The dying sun was still shining on the leaves, and the turtledoves in the birches sang their sweet, sad song.

Jorinda was struck with grief and began to weep, and Joringel, moved by the same feelings, also wept. They could not have felt more heavyhearted if they had been about to die. Now night was almost upon them. They looked around and no longer knew where they were, or how to reach home.

Joringel parted some bushes and saw that the crumbling castle walls were only a few steps away. His heart went cold with fear. Jorinda began to sing:

> "My little bird that's ringed with red
> Sings sorrow, sorrow, sorrow.
> It sings, 'The dove will soon be dead.
> Sing sorrow, sor—*jug, jug, tiroo, tiroo.*'"

Joringel turned toward her, but in her place was a nightingale, singing, "*Jug, jug, jug.*" A screech owl with eyes like glowing coals flew three times around the little bird, and three times cried, "*To-whoo, to-whoo, to-whoo.*"

Now Joringel could move neither hand nor foot. Stiff as a stone, he could neither speak nor weep.

The last of the sun went down, and the owl vanished into the thicket.

Seconds later, a bent old woman shuffled out. Her face was yellow and shrunken, her eyes were red as rubies, and her hooked nose met her chin. Muttering to herself, she caught the nightingale in her hands and was gone.

Left alone, still as a statue, Joringel could do nothing. But at last the witch returned and chanted out strange words: "I greet you, Zachiel. When the moon shines on the cage, free him, Zachiel."

Suddenly Joringel was free. He fell on his knees before the witch, begging her to give him back his love. But the witch gave a cackling laugh and scurried away. "You will never see her again!" she called back.

Joringel wept and pleaded, cursed and wailed, but all in vain. Unable to rest, he left the place where he had been born and wandered until he reached a village where no one knew him. There he stayed for many months, guarding sheep, telling no one his story. Often, though, he would go back to the forest and gaze at the witch's castle from a distance.

One night he had a dream. He dreamed that he found a flower as red as blood, with a drop of dew at its center like a perfect pearl. In his dream he plucked the flower and took it to the castle, where everything he touched with it was freed from the witch's spell. One of the maidens so restored was Jorinda, and she loved him as before.

When he awoke the next morning, he began to look for the flower. Far and wide he searched, for eight long days. Then at dawn on the ninth he found the bloodred flower. Plucking it carefully, he set out for the castle.

Now no evil magic could touch him, and he walked freely up to the door. He touched it with the flower and it sprang open. From room to room he went, until at last he found the one where the witch was feeding her prisoners in their seven thousand cages.

When the witch saw Joringel, her expression changed to one of fury. She spat gall and poison at him; she screamed and shouted curses; but try as she might, she could not touch the boy. Joringel took no notice, but went from cage to cage, looking at each bird. Oh, there were hundreds of nightingales. How was he ever to find Jorinda?

Suddenly looking up, he saw the old woman quietly creeping toward the door with a cage in her hand. He sprang forward and touched both the cage and the witch with the flower. The old woman's evil powers left her, and all the captive birds turned into girls. As for Jorinda, there she was—even lovelier than Joringel remembered. Hand in hand the two returned home, and they lived happily ever after.

The golden bird

LONG, LONG AGO, in a far-off time, there lived a king who had a beautiful garden just behind his palace. In it was a wondrous tree that grew golden apples. One day, when the apples were nearly ripe, they were counted.

The next morning, one was missing, so the king gave orders that an all-night watch must be kept until the thief was caught.

The king had three sons, and for the first watch he sent the eldest prince. But when midnight struck, the young man fell sound asleep. In the morning another apple had gone.

The next night, the second prince was sent to watch the tree. But he, too, slept, and when morning came, another apple was gone.

On the third night, the third prince begged to go. This youngest son was a bit of a dreamer, and the king didn't think much of him. But he hadn't much choice, so at last he let him have his way. The boy took care to keep awake, and when midnight struck something rushed like wind through the air, and the moonlight shone on a golden-feathered bird which alighted on the tree. The bird had just plucked an apple from a branch when the young prince shot at it with an arrow. The bird flew off, but one of its feathers was loosened and fell lightly to the ground.

In the morning, the boy took the feather to the king and told him what he had seen. The king showed the feather to his advisers, who all agreed that the feather was such a marvel that it was worth more than the entire kingdom.

"If one feather is so valuable," said the king, "I must have the bird itself."

And so the king sent his eldest son out to search for the golden bird. The prince was a conceited fellow, and was sure he'd find the creature easily. After traveling some miles, he saw a fox sitting at the edge of the wood. Immediately the prince raised his bow and took aim. But the fox called out, "Don't shoot me and I will give you some good advice. I know what you are here for; you are searching for the golden bird. This evening you will come to a village which has two inns on opposite sides of the road. One of the inns is warm and bright and filled with cheerful guests, but I tell you, don't stop there. Instead, go to the other inn; never mind if it looks dark and empty and glum."

"What nonsense," scoffed the prince, and shot the arrow. But the fox was too quick for him and disappeared into the woods.

The eldest son continued his journey, and at nightfall found himself at the village with the two inns, just as the fox had described them. What did he do? For all the fox's warning, the young man went to the one that was filled with noisy revelers. Once inside he joined the drinking, shouting crowd, and the golden bird and all his past vanished from his mind.

Time passed and no word came from the eldest son. So the second prince set out to find the magical bird. He, too, met the fox, and was given the same advice; he, too, reached the village with the inns. And there, at the window of the lively one, was his brother, calling him in. What did he do? He joined him, and once inside gave himself over to drinking and revelry, and everything else went out of his mind.

More time passed, and when no news came to the king from his elder sons, the youngest wanted to set out and try his luck. "If your brothers have failed," said the king, "how can you hope to do any better?" The king thought the boy a simpleton. But the young prince persisted, and at last the king let him go.

Once more the fox was waiting by the woods; once more he begged for his life and promised some good advice.

"Don't be afraid, little fox," said the prince. "I won't hurt you."

Then the fox told him about the two village inns. "To save you time," he added, "get on my tail and I'll take you there myself."

The prince climbed onto the long bushy tail and the fox sped away, over hill and dale, through bush and briar, so fast that the prince's hair whistled in the wind. They reached the village. The prince dismounted, and without looking around, entered the quiet inn, where he spent a peaceful night.

In the morning, he restarted his journey and, just outside the village, who should he see but the fox. "Now," said the fox, "I see that you are a sensible lad. So I'm going to tell you what to do next. You go straight ahead, on and on, until you come to a castle. A regiment of soldiers will be lying in front, but don't worry, they'll all be sound asleep. Just walk right through and into the castle. Go through all the rooms and in the very last you'll see a golden bird in a wooden cage. Nearby you'll see another cage made all of gold. Whatever happens, don't take the bird out of the wooden cage and put it in the golden one, or you'll really be in trouble. Now get on." And he stretched out his tail

and carried the prince over hill and dale at such a speed that the boy's hair whistled in the wind.

When he reached the castle, the youngest son found everything just as the fox had said. He went through the sleeping soldiers and found the room with the golden bird in a plain wooden cage, and a cage of gold hanging beside it. The three missing golden apples were scattered on the floor. But the prince didn't like to see that beautiful bird in such a common cage, so he lifted it out and put it into the golden one. At once the bird uttered a piercing scream. The sleeping soldiers woke, rushed in, and carried off the prince to a prison cell under the palace.

The next morning the prince was sentenced to death. But the king gave him a chance to save his life. "Bring me back the golden horse which can run faster than the wind," pronounced the king, "and you shall have your freedom and the golden bird as well."

The prince set off with a heavy heart. Where in all the regions of the world would he find the golden horse? But then he saw the friendly fox sitting by the side of the road. "Well, well," said the fox, "see what happens when you don't follow my advice! Now listen this time, and I'll tell you what to do. Go straight ahead, on and on, and you'll come to a castle. In the stable there's a golden horse. The grooms will all be sound asleep, and you can lead the horse out quite easily without disturbing them. That is, if you remember one thing. You must put the plain wood and leather saddle on the horse, and not the golden one which hangs nearby, or you'll find yourself in trouble. Don't forget!"

Then the fox stretched out his tail, the king's son seated himself upon it, and they raced away, over hill and dale, through bush and briar, until the prince's hair flew whistling in the wind.

Yes, everything was just as the fox had said, the castle and the sleeping grooms and the stable with the golden horse. But the prince thought that the wood and leather saddle didn't look good enough for that beautiful creature, and he took down the golden one instead. No sooner did it touch the horse's

back, however, than a tremendous whinnying came from the animal. The grooms rushed in and seized the prince and locked him in a cell. The next morning he was again sentenced to death, but the king offered the youth a chance to save his life. "If you bring me back the princess from the golden castle," said the king, "I will give you both your freedom and the golden horse."

The young prince was quite down in the dumps when he set out. How was he to find this beautiful girl? But there by the roadside was the helpful fox. "I really ought to leave you to your own foolishness," said the fox, "but I'm a good-natured soul, and I'll give you one more chance. This path goes straight to the golden castle, but it's a long way off, and you won't get there until evening. Then you must hide and wait until midnight, when everyone is asleep; that's when the princess goes to the bathing house. Run to her, give her a kiss, and she will follow you. But remember this—you must not let her say good-bye to her parents, or you'll find yourself in trouble, I can tell you."

When the prince reached the golden castle, everything was just as the fox had said. He waited until midnight, when all was quiet, and then he saw the princess come to the bathing house. He sprang out from his hiding place and kissed her and sure enough she agreed to go with him without a word of protest. But she did want to say good-bye to her parents first.

The prince remembered the fox's words, and three times refused to grant her request. But she wept and pleaded and knelt before him until he had to give in. No sooner had the princess reached her parents' bedside than everyone within the castle awoke. The prince was seized and thrown into a cell.

The next morning, the prince was sentenced to death, but the king made him an offer. "You see that mountain blocking the view from my window?" said the monarch. "If you can move it within eight days, you can have your freedom and marry my daughter as well."

The prince began to dig and dig. Yet after seven days' hard toil, the mountain looked as solid as before, and he really felt that all his hope was gone. But on the night of the seventh day the fox turned up. "You don't deserve any more help from me," he said. "I must be as big a fool as you are to bother with you still. But I'll give you one more chance. Go to sleep, and I'll get busy. Tomorrow you will see what you will see."

The fox was as good as his word. The next morning when the prince woke up, where was the mountain? It had disappeared completely. The king had to keep his promise, and the prince set out on his journey back with the beautiful princess.

They had not gone far when they met the faithful fox. "Well," he said, "you have done better than I would have expected, but you're not yet out of the wood. Now listen carefully. Take the princess to the king who sent you to find her. He will be overjoyed and he'll have the golden horse brought out to you. As soon as they bring the horse into the courtyard, mount him, then offer your hand to everyone in farewell. Last of all, hold out your hand to the princess; then you must swing her up behind you and speed away. No one will be able to catch you, for that horse can travel faster than the wind."

All went just as the fox had said, and there was the prince on the road again, with the golden horse as well as the fair princess.

The fox was waiting for him. "So far, so good," he said. "Now I will tell you how to get the golden bird. When you come to the castle where the bird is kept, set the princess down from the horse and I will take her into my care. Then ride into the courtyard. The king will be more than happy to see you, and will have the golden bird brought out. As soon as you have the cage in your hand, gallop away on the horse to this place where we will be waiting for you."

The prince did as the fox said, and soon he was safely away with the princess, the horse, and the golden bird. But when he was saying good-bye to his friend, the fox said, "And now you must reward me for my help."

"But of course," cried the prince. "Anything you want is yours."

"This is what I want," said the fox. "When we reach that forest over there, you must kill me and chop off my head and my feet."

The prince, however, was shocked at this request. "What sort of gratitude is that?" he said. "I could not possibly do such a terrible thing."

"Ah, well," said the fox. "If you will not help me, I will have to leave you. But I will give you one last piece of advice—make sure that you buy no gallows' meat and take care not to sit at the edge of any well." Then he vanished into the woods.

That is a marvelous creature, the young man thought to himself, but he has some strange whims. Why should I buy gallows' meat? Or sit at the edge of a well? And he rode on with the princess until they came to the village of the two inns.

Something unusual was happening; the streets were full of crowds and noise. He asked a passerby what was going on. "Oh, a couple of scoundrels are going to be hanged," he was told.

Then, as the prince came near to the gallows, he saw that the two men were his brothers. They had been up to all kinds of wickedness. "Is there no way those men could be set free?" he asked a guard.

"You can buy them off if you like," said the guard. "But they are rotten rubbish, the pair of them, and would be a waste of your money."

The prince didn't stop to think. He paid what he was asked; his brothers were freed, and they all rode off together.

At last they came to the wood where they had first met the fox. The day was hot, and the brothers suggested that they rest in the cool by a well that was near at hand. Once more the youngest brother forgot to be on his guard, and sat down on the rim. Instantly his brothers jumped to their feet and threw him backward into the depths below. Then they took the princess, the golden horse and the golden bird, and went home to their father. "Look," they cried. "Not only have we brought you the golden bird as you asked, but the princess from the golden castle and the golden horse as well."

The king was overjoyed to see them. But as time went on, the horse refused to eat, the bird refused to sing, and the princess sat and wept both day and night.

Now, in spite of his brothers' villainy, the young prince was not dead. The well into which he fell was dry, and he landed on a bed of good soft moss. Try as he might, however, he could not get out. He had just resigned himself to a lonely death when the fox looked down from above.

"Will you never listen to what I say?" said the fox. "Still, I can't leave you here. Take hold of my tail and I'll pull you out." And that's what he did. "You are not safe yet, though," said the fox. "Your brothers aren't taking any chances; their spies are everywhere, all through the forest, ready to kill you if they find you alive." So the fox disguised the prince as a poor man, and together they journeyed back to the prince's home.

It seemed that no one in the palace recognized the young prince. But suddenly, the golden bird began to sing, the horse began to eat, and the beautiful princess smiled for the first time. The king was amazed. "What's the reason for all this?" he asked.

"I don't know," said the princess, "but I feel as if my true bridegroom has come at last." And then she told him all that had happened.

The king ordered everyone in the palace to come before him, and among them was the prince in his ragged clothes. As soon as the princess saw him, she threw herself into his arms.

The evil brothers were seized and put to death. The prince married his princess, and the king declared him heir to the throne and kingdom.

Have you forgotten the fox? Listen now. One day the prince was walking in the forest when he saw his faithful friend. "You have everything now that you could ever wish for," said the fox. "But I am under a wretched spell which you alone can break." And again he begged the prince to kill him and to chop off his head and feet. This time the prince did so. At once the fox changed into a handsome young man, the brother of the princess herself, freed at last from the magic spell that had been cast on him. Now their happiness was complete, and it lasted as long as they lived.

The three little men
in the wood

THERE WAS ONCE a man whose wife had died and left him with a
daughter to bring up. And there was once a woman whose husband had
died and left her with a daughter to bring up. The two girls knew one another
and went out for a walk. Then they returned to the woman's house, and the
woman said to her daughter's friend, "Tell your father that I would like to
marry him and be a mother to you. Tell him that when we are married, you
shall wash yourself in milk every day and your drink shall be wine. But my
own daughter shall wash herself in water and water shall be her drink."

The girl went home and told her father what the woman had said. "Well, I
don't know," said the father. "Marriage can be a joy, but it can also be a
torment."

At last, since he couldn't make up his mind, he pulled off his boot and
handed it to his daughter. "Look," he said, "this boot has a hole. Take the boot,
hang it on a nail, and pour in a bucket of water. If it holds the water, then I'll
marry. If the water runs through it, I won't. That should settle that."

The girl took the boot up to the loft, hung it on a nail, and filled it with water. But the water drew the hole together and not one drop escaped.

When the girl told her father, he refused to believe her. He went to see for himself—and there it was! Well, what could he do but go along to the widow, and that's how they came to get married.

The day after the wedding there was milk for the man's daughter to wash in and wine for her to drink—but for the woman's daughter there was water to wash in and water to drink, just as the widow had promised.

On the second morning, there was water for washing and water for drinking for both of them. And on the third morning there was water for washing and water for drinking for the man's daughter—and milk for washing and wine for drinking for the woman's daughter. And that's how it went on. For the woman loathed her stepdaughter, who was so pretty and good-natured that everyone loved her, but nobody liked her own daughter, who was both ugly and mean.

One winter's day, when the earth itself was frozen as hard as stone and every hill and vale lay covered in snow, the woman called her stepdaughter and handed her a paper dress she had made. "Here," she said, "put on this dress; go out into the woods and bring me back this basket filled with strawberries. I have a craving for them."

The girl was puzzled. "But strawberries don't grow in the dead of winter!" she said. "The ground is frozen solid and everything is covered with snow. And why must I wear this thin paper dress? The wind will blow right through it and the thorns will tear it to pieces."

"How dare you argue with me," said the woman. "Is that all the thanks I get for giving you bed and board? Now be off. I don't want to see your face again until you bring back the fruit."

Then she gave the girl a piece of stale bread, saying, "Here's your food for the day. It will last you until you get back." But she privately thought that the girl would die of hunger and cold, and that she would never see her again.

The girl put on the paper dress, took up the basket, and went out into the woods. Nothing but snow could she see, not so much as a single blade of grass. Then between the trees she saw a tiny house, and peering out from it were three little men. So she curtsied and knocked shyly at the door.

"Come in!" they cried together. "Come in!"

She thanked them, entered the tiny room, and sat down on a bench by the stove to warm herself. Then she took out her piece of bread.

"Give us some!" cried the little men. "Give us some!"

"Of course," said the girl. She broke her bread in two and gave them half.

"What are you doing out here in the wood, with that paper dress, in all this ice and snow?" they asked the girl.

"My stepmother has sent me out," she replied, "to fill this basket with strawberries. I am not to return without them."

When the girl had eaten her bread, the dwarfs gave her a broom and told her to sweep away the snow at the back door. As soon as she had gone outside, the three little men began to discuss what they should give her for being so good and kind, and for sharing her bread with them.

The first dwarf said, "My gift is that every day she will become more beautiful."

The second dwarf said, "My gift is that a gold coin will fall from her mouth every time she speaks."

The third dwarf said, "My gift is that a king will come and take her as his wife."

The girl knew nothing of this. She swept the snow from behind the little house, and there beneath the icy flakes what did she see but a patch of ripe red strawberries growing from the ground. Joyfully she gathered them into her basket, thanked the little men, clasped the hand of each, and hurried home.

But when she began to tell what had happened, with every word she uttered a gold coin dropped from her mouth.

"What arrogance," cried the stepsister, running her hands through the coins on the floor, "to throw money around like this." But really she longed to go to the forest herself, to have the same good luck. However, when she asked her mother if she could go, the woman said, "No, no, it is far too cold; you would freeze to death."

Still the daughter begged and begged, until at last the woman gave her consent. But she made her wear a warm fur cloak and carry with her a good supply of bread and butter and cake. The girl marched into the forest and made straight for the tiny house. The three little men peeped out as they had done before, but she did not greet them politely, nor did she bother to knock. She barged right into the room, seated herself at the stove, and began to eat her meal.

"Give us some!" cried the three little men. But the girl refused.

"Why should I?" she said. "There isn't even enough for me."

After she had finished eating, they said to her, "Take this broom and sweep the ground outside the back door."

"Sweep it yourselves," she said. "I'm no servant!" But at last, when nothing happened, she sulkily got to her feet and thumped out with the broom.

Now the three little men discussed what they should give her in return for her rudeness and greed.

The first dwarf said, "My gift to her is that she will become uglier and uglier every day."

The second dwarf said, "My gift is that a toad will jump from her mouth every time she speaks."

The third said, "My gift to her is that she will die the death she deserves."

Meanwhile the girl poked around for strawberries. When she found nothing but snow and ice, she stomped off home. But every time she opened her mouth to tell her mother what had happened, a toad sprang out. And people thought her even nastier than before.

The stepdaughter, though, grew more and more beautiful every day, and every day the woman's hatred increased. Morning, noon, and night she thought of nothing else but a way to do her stepchild harm.

At last she boiled some yarn in an old pot, and when it was done she threw it over the girl's shoulder, handed her an axe, and told her to go to the frozen river, cut a hole in the ice, and rinse the yarn.

The obedient girl went to the river and tried to chop a hole in the ice. While she was doing this a magnificent carriage came by and a king was sitting inside. He stopped the carriage and asked the girl, "Who are you, child? What are you doing here?"

"I am a poor girl," she replied, "and I am trying to rinse this yarn for my stepmother."

The king was moved by her words and her sweet voice. Then, when she looked up, he was struck by her extraordinary beauty. "Would you like to come with me?" he said.

"Most gladly," she answered, for she longed to escape from her cruel mother and sister.

So she stepped into the carriage. It rolled away, and when they reached the royal palace, they had a magnificent wedding, just as the dwarf had promised. At the end of the year the young queen gave birth to a son, a little prince.

The stepmother came to hear of this and how the king had met his bride while she was rinsing yarn in the river, and she realized what had happened. So she and her daughter went to visit the queen at the palace, and they were kindly received. But one morning when the king was away and no one about, they

seized the queen and flung her out of the window into the stream below. Then the ugly daughter got into the royal bed and the old woman drew the covers over her head. When the king returned and wanted to speak to his wife, the stepmother said, "No, no, she has a fever and needs to rest tonight."

The next morning, he came in and spoke to the invalid. But a toad came out of her mouth when she answered, instead of a gold piece. "That's only her fever," said the old woman. "She'll soon be better."

But during the night, the kitchen boy saw a duck swimming in the moat. The duck cried:

"O husband king, O husband king,
I call, but get no answering."

The boy didn't know what to say. Then the duck spoke again:

"What are my servants all about?"

The boy replied:

"They're all asleep, you needn't doubt."

Then the duck said:

"Why do I hear my baby crying?"

The boy replied:

"He's wakeful, in his cradle lying."

Then the duck took on human shape—she was the queen. She went upstairs, nursed her baby, plumped his pillows, and tucked him in. After this she went back to the water and was once again a duck.

For two nights she visited in this way, but on the third night she said to the kitchen boy, "Go tell the king to take his sword, stand on the threshold, and swing it over me three times."

The boy obeyed, and the king picked up his sword and followed the boy outside. When he had swung the sword three times over the duck, his wife stood before him, as well and lovely as ever. The king was overcome with joy, but this quickly turned to rage when he heard her story. He decided to keep his queen well hidden until the day of the christening.

After the christening of the prince, the king said to his mother-in-law, "What punishment does a person deserve who tries to kill another by drowning?"

"Why," cried the woman, "such a one should be thrown in a barrel with nails and rolled into the water."

"You have described your own sentence," said the king. And the woman and her daughter were put into just such a barrel. It was rolled into the river and was gone.

Snow White

ONCE LONG AGO, in the middle of winter, when snowflakes drifted down from the sky like feathers, a queen sat sewing by a window which was framed with ebony. As she looked up from her sewing to gaze at the falling flakes, she pricked her finger with the needle and three drops of blood fell down onto the snow. The red drops looked so beautiful on the snow that she said to herself, "Ah, if only I had a child who was as white as snow, as red as blood, and as black as the wood of this window frame!"

Soon after that, the queen gave birth to a daughter whose skin was as white

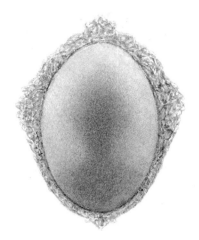

as snow, whose lips were as red as blood, and whose hair was as black as ebony, and the little princess was called Snow White. But when the child was born, the queen died.

A year passed, and the king took another wife. She was a beautiful woman, but proud and haughty, and she couldn't endure the thought that anyone else might be more beautiful than she. Every day she would stand before her magic mirror, saying,

> "Mirror, mirror, on the wall,
> Who is the fairest one of all?"

And every day the mirror would answer,

> "Queen, Queen, fair Queen,
> In me the truth is seen.
> Rival beauty is there none—
> You are still the fairest one."

This made the queen feel content, since she knew that the mirror had to speak the truth.

But as Snow White grew, so did her beauty. By the time she was seven years old, she was as beautiful as the day, more beautiful even than the queen herself.

One morning, when the queen asked,

> "Mirror, mirror, on the wall,
> Who is the fairest one of all?"

the mirror answered,

"You are fair as fair can be,
But young Snow White is more fair than thee."

The queen turned yellow and green with rage and fury, and from that hour on, whenever she saw Snow White, her hatred made her heart turn over within her.

Her pride and envy grew and grew and gripped her heart like weeds; she could think of nothing else. At last, she sent for a huntsman. "Take that child into the forest and get rid of her," she said. "And bring me back her lungs and liver so that I know you've done it."

The hunter set off with the little princess, but when he reached the woods and drew his knife, the girl began to weep. "Good huntsman, let me live," she begged. "I'll run off into the forest and never come back, I promise you."

Because she was so beautiful, the huntsman took pity on her. "All right, you poor little thing, run away," he said, and he thought to himself, Well, the wild beasts will probably deal with her.

Then a young boar appeared. The huntsman killed it, cut out its lungs and liver, and took them to the queen as proof that the girl was dead. The queen was delighted. She ordered the cook to salt and stew these entrails, and ate them for her dinner, thinking that they came from the dead Snow White.

Snow White was alive, however, but she was all alone in the great forest, with its rustling leaves and darkness, and she wept with terror because she didn't know what to do. She began to run in all directions, paying no attention to the sharp stones underfoot and the tearing thorns and brambles. The wild beasts saw her pass but did nothing to harm her. She ran and ran till her legs would scarcely carry her and then, when the day had almost gone, she came to a little house.

Everything in the house was tiny, but as neat and clean as could be. There was a tiny table covered with a white cloth, and on the table were seven little plates, with knife, fork, and spoon by each, and seven little mugs. Against the opposite wall were seven little beds in a neat row, each one covered with a clean, white counterpane.

Snow White was so hungry and thirsty that she helped herself to a few

vegetables and bits of bread from each plate, and a drop of wine from each mug. Then she went to lie down and rest. She tried one bed after the other; one was too long, one was too short, and only the seventh was just right. She said her prayers, lay down, and quickly fell asleep.

When night came, the owners of the little house came home. They were seven dwarfs who went out every day to mine silver in the mountains. Each dwarf lit a candle, and now they could see that someone had been there—things weren't as tidy as when they had left the place.

"Who has been sitting on my chair?" asked the first dwarf.

The second said, "Who has been eating from my plate?"

"Who has nibbled my bread?" said the third.

The fourth said, "Who has been tasting my vegetables?"

The fifth said, "Who has used my fork?"

"Who has cut with my knife?" said the sixth.

"Someone has drunk from my cup," said the seventh.

Then the first dwarf saw a hollow in his bed. "Who has been lying here?" he said. The others ran up and looked, saying, "Someone has been in my bed."

But the seventh dwarf saw that someone was still there. It was Snow White.

All the dwarfs crowded around her with their little candles. "Oh my, my," they whispered. "What a lovely child!" And they tucked the cover around her chin and tiptoed away. The seventh dwarf slept in turn with the others, an hour with each, and then it was morning.

The daylight woke Snow White. She was quite frightened to see the dwarfs, but they said "Good morning" to her most politely, and asked her name.

"My name is Snow White," she said. And she told them all about her stepmother and the plan to have her killed, and about the hunter and her flight through the forest, and how she had found the little house. Then the dwarfs spoke to each other, and turned to the little girl—"If you will take care of our home while we are at work, and cook and make the beds and wash and sew and see that everything is neat and clean, you can stay with us and you'll want for nothing."

"I will gladly do that," said Snow White.

So she stayed and kept the house in order, and every morning the little men went off to the mountains, and every evening they would return and find their dinner ready. The dwarfs grew very fond of Snow White, and she grew fond of them. But the dwarfs still worried that she was alone all day. "Watch out for that stepmother of yours," they said. "She's bound to discover what has happened, and she'll be on your trail at once. So don't let anyone in while we're away, not anyone."

Now when the queen had eaten the lungs and liver, she felt sure that she was once again the most beautiful woman in the land. She went to the mirror, saying,

"Mirror, mirror, on the wall,
Who is the fairest one of all?"

But the reply was not what she had expected:

"O Queen, fair Queen,
In me the truth is seen;
In the woods, where dwarf-kind dwell,
Snow White is alive and well.
You are as lovely as the sun
But Snow White is the lovelier one."

The queen was devoured with rage. She knew now that the huntsman had deceived her and that Snow White was still alive, and she thought of nothing else, night and day.

At last, she thought of a plan to destroy the girl. Disguising herself as an old peddler woman, she left the castle and journeyed over the seven mountains to the house of the seven dwarfs. Then she knocked at the door, crying out, "Pretty things for sale! Pretty things for sale!"

Snow White looked out of the window. "Good day, old lady. What have you to sell?" she asked.

"Good things, lovely things," said the old woman. "Ribbons and lacing of every color!" And she brought out some fine silk lacings from her bag. Snow White thought there could be no harm in letting in this good old woman, so she unbolted the door and bought the lace.

"Oh, you poor child," said the woman.

"Your clothes look terrible. Come here, and I'll do you up properly."

So Snow White let the old woman thread the new ribbons in her bodice. But the woman worked fast, and pulled the laces so tight that Snow White could not breathe, and she fell to the floor as if dead.

"Well," said the woman, "you may have been the fairest once, but you are not that now. I am." And she hurried off.

When the seven dwarfs returned home that evening, they were horrified to see Snow White lying on the floor, and they thought she must be dead. But when they lifted her up and saw the tight lacing, they loosened it and she slowly returned to life. Soon she was well enough to tell them all that had happened.

"That peddler woman was the wicked queen, you can be sure of that," said the dwarfs. "She'll be up to her tricks again before long, that's certain. Now remember, don't let anyone in at all while we are away—not anyone."

As soon as she was back in the castle, the queen threw off her disguise and stood before the mirror, saying,

"Mirror, mirror, on the wall,
Who is the fairest one of all?"

But the mirror only answered as it had before,
"O Queen, fair Queen,
In me the truth is seen;
In the woods, where dwarf-kind
    dwell,
Snow White is alive and well.
You are lovely as the sun
But Snow White is the lovelier one."

All the blood seemed to rush from the queen's heart. "I'll think of something to put an end to her once and for all," she declared, and she used her knowledge of witchery to make a poisoned comb. Then, disguising herself as another old woman, she made the journey back to the home of the seven dwarfs.

"Pretty things for sale!" she called at the door. "Pretty things for a pretty girl!"

Snow White looked out of the window. "Go away!" she said. "I mustn't let anyone in."

The old woman smiled and said, "There's no harm in just looking, is there?" And at last she held up the beautiful, poisoned comb.

Snow White was so beguiled by it that again she forgot the warnings of the dwarfs and opened the door. When they had made a bargain, the old woman said, "Your hair needs a proper combing, child. Come, I'll do it for you."

So Snow White stood for the woman to do her hair, but no sooner had the comb touched her than the poison took effect, and she fell senseless to the floor.

"That should finish you," cried the queen, with a wild laugh. "You're done for now." And off she went.

When the seven dwarfs returned home, they saw Snow White lying pale and still on the ground, and they were pretty sure the queen had been back again. Seeing the comb still in her hair, they pulled it out, and immediately the girl began to recover and told them what had happened.

"You must listen to us, Snow White," they told her. "Don't let anyone in while we're gone, not anyone."

When the queen reached the palace she went at once to her mirror, saying,

"Mirror, mirror, on the wall,
Who is the fairest one of all?"

But the mirror answered,

"O Queen, fair Queen,
In me the truth is seen;
In the woods, where dwarf-kind
   dwell,
Snow White is alive and well.
You are lovely as the sun
But Snow White is the lovelier
   one."

The queen shook from head to foot. "Snow White must die," she raged. "Even if it costs me my life!" Then she went into a secret room, unknown to any but herself, and made a poison apple, very nice to look at, red on one side and white on the other, but on the red side, even the smallest bite would bring death. Then she disguised herself as a poor peasant woman, and went once more to the house of the dwarfs. She knocked on the door, and Snow White put her head out of the window.

"You must go away," said the girl. "I'm not allowed to let anyone in."

The old woman laughed. "Don't tell me you're afraid of being poisoned. Look, I'll cut the apple in two. You can have the red half and I'll have the white." She took a bite from her own half and handed the poisoned half to the girl.

Snow White could not resist the fresh-looking fruit. She raised the apple to her lips, but no sooner had she taken one bite than she fell dead to the floor.

The queen gave a shout of terrible laughter. "White as snow, red as blood, black as ebony, you shall not wake this time!" Then she sped back to the palace and raced to the mirror, saying,

"Mirror, mirror, on the wall,
Who is the fairest one of all?"

And the mirror answered,

"O Queen, fair Queen,
In me the truth is seen.
Snow White sleeps. The deed is done.
You are now the fairest one."

And so for the time being her jealous heart was calm.

When the dwarfs returned home in the evening, they found Snow White motionless on the floor. They lifted her to the bed, they looked for poisoned trinkets, loosened her clothes, but it was all of no use. She was dead.

They laid her upon a bier, and for three long days they sat around it and wept. At last, it was time to bury her. But she still looked alive.

"We can't put her in the dark ground," they said. And they made a coffin of glass, so that she could be seen from every side, and wrote her name in gold, saying that she was the daughter of a king. They set the coffin on a hill, and they took turns to stand guard by it day and night. Birds came to visit and sing for the princess: first an owl, then a raven, and lastly a dove.

Snow White lay in her coffin a long, long time. She did not change but looked as though she were only sleeping. Her skin remained as white as snow, her lips as red as blood, and her hair as black as ebony.

One day a young prince rode by, saw the coffin of glass with the beautiful girl inside, and read the words of gold. He said to the dwarfs, "She is the most beautiful girl I have ever seen. Let me have the coffin, and I will give you whatever you ask."

But there was nothing that the dwarfs wanted. "We will not part with her for all the gold in the world," they said.

"Then let me have it as a gift," said the prince, "for I cannot live without seeing Snow White. I will honor and love her as though she were still alive."

The dwarfs took pity on him and let him take the coffin. But as the prince's men were carrying it away on their shoulders, they stumbled over a tree stump, and the jolting shook the coffin so much that the piece of poisoned

99

apple came out of Snow White's throat. She opened her eyes and sat up with a cry. "Where am I?" she asked.

"You are with me," said the prince. Then he told her all that had happened. "I love you more than anything in the world," he said. "Come with me to my father's castle and be my wife."

Snow White went with him, for she loved him too, and wedding celebrations of great magnificence were announced through the land.

Now one of the guests invited was the wicked queen. Before she left, dressed in her most beautiful clothes, she stood as usual before the mirror, saying,

"Mirror, mirror, on the wall,
Who is the fairest one of all?"

And the mirror answered,

"O Queen, fair Queen,
In me the truth is seen.
No one is as fair as you,
Except Snow White, a queen now too."

The queen was so struck with horror that she didn't know what to do next. But at last her curiosity got the better of her and she decided to go to the wedding to see the bride for herself. The moment she entered the ball she recognized Snow White. But she could not escape. Red hot iron shoes were put on her feet and she was made to dance until she fell down dead.